Murder at Mistletoe Manor: A Mystery Novella

Book 1 in the Windy Pines Mystery Series

by Holly Tierney-Bedord

Also by Holly Tierney-Bedord

Bellamy's Redemption

Carnage at the Christmas Party:
Book 2 in the Windy Pines Mystery Series

Coached

The Magical Power of Butter Cookies

Right Under Your Nose: A Christmas Story

Ring in the New Year

Run Away Baby

The Snowflake Valley Advice Fairy

Sunflowers and Second Chances

Surviving Valencia

Weekend Immune System

Zeke and Angelique

Cover design by Holly Tierney-Bedord, featuring artwork from Adobe Stock.

Murder at Mistletoe Manor: A Mystery Novella,

by Holly Tierney-Bedord

copyright © 2016 by Holly Tierney-Bedord.

Excerpt from *Right Under Your Nose: A Christmas Story* by Holly Tierney-Bedord

copyright © 2015 by Holly Tierney-Bedord.

ISBN: 9781519012678

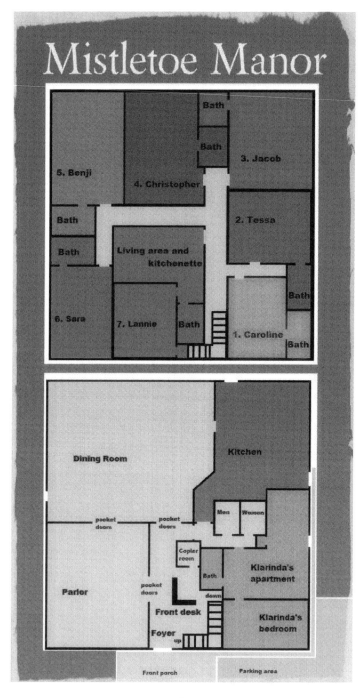

Chapter 1

There were seven guestrooms at Mistletoe Manor, and it was strange for more than one to be booked on a Tuesday in December. Yet here was the appointment book with all rooms confirmed, a week in advance, no less.

Klarinda Snow chewed on the eraser of her pencil, pondering the odds. Unable to make sense of this anomaly, she brought up the Windy Pines online calendar of events to see if there was something special going on around town that night. Aside from the Christmas market, which happened throughout the holiday season, there was nothing special on the calendar.

"Must be some kind of a reunion," she said aloud. But if it was a reunion, wouldn't at least one of the guests have said so? And wouldn't they have booked their rooms all together, at once? But she could tell from the different colors of ink in the appointment book that Myrtle had written them at separate times. She flipped the page over to the notes section, but there was nothing written there.

Just then the door swung open and her Jill-of-all-trades came in, carrying a pile of snow-dusted firewood.

"Hello, Klarinda! It's getting nasty out there!" Myrtle said, setting the pile of wood on the old bench just inside the foyer by the front door. She removed her mittens and hat and set them on the radiator. "Do you want the fireplace in the dining room going yet, or should we hold off until later in the day?"

"Let's hold off for now," said Klarinda, anxious to ration as much firewood as possible. Unfortunately, running Mistletoe Manor meant scrimping on the luxuries, and sometimes even the necessities, at all times. "Myrtle, did all these bookings for December thirteenth come in at the same time?"

"Throughout the day yesterday, when you were up in Winter River getting new snow tires put on your truck."

"Seems a little funny to have every room booked, doesn't it?"

"I certainly thought so," said Myrtle.

"And none of them paid in advance?"

"Come to think of it, I guess not."

"Strange. We may need to change our policy on allowing bookings without prepayment. I feel like we're being scammed," said Klarinda.

"You're such a cynic," joked Myrtle.

"Perhaps. Or maybe I'm a realist. Did any of them mention one another?"

"No. Each seemed to be unrelated and random. It happens, I suppose. All the rooms getting booked at once like that."

"It *doesn't* happen, though," said Klarinda. "I wish it did! But I can't remember the last time all seven rooms were booked at once."

"Don't look down on good luck," Myrtle advised.

"I'm not," said Klarinda, smiling to prove it. Nearly twenty years younger than Myrtle, she received her fair share of sometimes-wise and often-overbearing pearls of wisdom from the older woman, despite that she was Myrtle's boss. Still, she appreciated Myrtle's work ethic and experience, so she usually bit her tongue when Myrtle doled out her advice. Not to mention, sometimes Myrtle was right.

"Oh, bother! This means we're going to have to get the toilet working in the purple guestroom," said Myrtle, remembering the project Klarinda had been reminding her about for two months.

"So... You got that?" asked Klarinda.

"Yes, boss. I got it," said Myrtle, shaking her head good-naturedly. "While I take care of that, you need to call The Christmas Company. They can bring a tree here, with lights and non-breakable red ornaments, and have it all set up for just two hundred ninety-nine dollars. It could be here by the end of the business day today."

"Nice try," said Klarinda, "but it's not in our budget."

"You're the boss," sighed Myrtle.

With Myrtle upstairs, plunging away, or whatever it was she was doing, Klarinda went back to the appointment book, checking to see if any of the names were familiar to her.

In the master suite at the front of the inn were Alanna Winthorpe-Newcastle and Tom Newcastle. In the yellow room at the front corner of the inn, was Caroline Bradbury, alone. In the blue room across the hall from her was Tessa Wycliffe, also alone. Next were Jacob Reese in the green room and Christopher Murdock across the hall from him in the gray room. The last two rooms were the least used, often unbooked for weeks on end. Benji McKellar had reserved the orange room and Sara Byers was across the hall in the purple room. Klarinda didn't recognize any of these names as those of previous visitors.

"Seems a little strange that single people have booked six of our seven rooms," Klarinda noted aloud to herself. Mistletoe Manor was, unquestionably, a romantic escape for couples. There were no conference centers or large corporations in the tiny mountain town of Windy Pines, population 3,259. It was nearly twenty miles from the closest large highway, and forty miles from the nearest small airport. This wasn't the kind of town or inn where people came for business, or while stopping off in the middle of traveling. It was a destination in itself, and single bookings were rare.

Befuddled, she closed the appointment book and headed back to the kitchen to check on Pierre, her chef. On slow days like this, he only made soup and a couple varieties of sandwiches for lunch, and a few pasta dishes and steak for dinner. Weather permitting, the Windy Pines Bake Shoppe brought in fresh bread and rolls each morning. Despite the limited menu, the inn's dining room was considered the best restaurant in all of Windy Pines.

"Did Myrtle mention to you that we have a full house next week?" Klarinda asked Pierre.

"Can't say that she did," said Pierre. "You mean next *weekend*?"

"Next Tuesday, actually. The night of the thirteenth."

"What's the occasion? Some kind of family reunion?"

"I don't think so," said Klarinda.

"One of those ladies' crafting parties?" asked Pierre, offering Klarinda a taste of some new salad dressing he had created earlier in the day to go with the evening's menu.

She nodded in approval. "Good stuff. But no, it doesn't look that way either. Maybe it's just a coincidence."

"You think so?" asked Pierre, unable to hide his skepticism. He looked around them at the empty dining room. They hadn't had more than three or four tables filled at one time since late September.

"I don't know, Pierre. It's weird, but I ought to be excited about it. We certainly need the business around here."

"You can say that again," said Pierre. Like Myrtle, he was single, in his fifties, and lived on the premises, in one of the two apartments in the old carriage house behind the inn. Neither he nor Myrtle had gotten a raise in years. When Klarinda purchased the inn two years earlier she'd been lucky enough to inherit Pierre and Myrtle... along with all the items she *hadn't* been lucky to inherit. Like a leaky roof, outdated furniture, and atrocious utility bills. She'd had big dreams of freshening up the inn, advertising more, and turning it into the showcase she knew it could be. After all, it was a beautiful old inn in a picturesque setting. But so far, she'd only gotten as far as reshingling the roof, purchasing some new bedding, and creating a new website for the inn. Now, out of extra money, she was waiting for a miracle. Perhaps all these guests showing up at once were the start of that.

"You know we've got a big storm rolling in on Tuesday night," said Pierre.

"Which means they may all end up canceling," said Klarinda.

"Or, if you're really lucky, maybe they'll all stay another night."

"Wouldn't that be something?" All seven rooms booked for two nights in a row could mean getting the snow blower they needed and some new drapes for the dining room, and maybe even a new toilet for the purple room's bathroom. "Running an inn certainly isn't as romantic as people think it is," Klarinda remarked.

Pierre raised his potato masher and sighed. "Tell me about it."

Chapter 2

"This place isn't as nice in person as the website makes it look," said the tall, blonde woman standing before the reception desk. To prove her point, she strutted over to the staircase and ran her finger along an obscure little groove in the detailing of the woodwork, producing a small pile of dust. She strutted back to the front desk, held the bit of gray fluff in front of Klarinda's face, and then softly blew it onto the floor.

"Uh, well, I'm sorry you feel that way," Klarinda stammered. "And sorry about that dust. There's a lot to keep up with here." She glanced over the woman's shoulder through the front window, as the Newtown Airport Taxi that had just dropped her off turned right out of the inn's parking lot. Large flakes of snow were just beginning to fall.

"Caroline Bradbury. I'm here for one night."

"Welcome, Caroline. Could I see your credit card and driver's license, please?" asked Klarinda.

"You need my credit card?"

"And your license, please."

"You need them *both*? Fine. Whatever." Caroline reached into her handbag, pulled out her matching wallet, removed a credit card and her driver's license, and tossed both onto the counter in front of Klarinda.

"Thank you. I'll be right back with these," said Klarinda, going off to make photocopies of them. It was probably illegal, but it had been the way the last owners did it, and it was how she did it now.

"Is there someone who can take my luggage? I'm tired of hauling it around," Caroline yelled to the empty lobby of the inn, while Klarinda stood waiting for the copier to warm up.

"Yes," she called back, over her shoulder, "if you don't mind waiting just a minute, Ms. Bradbury." Her voice sounded much more pleasant than she actually felt.

"It's *incredibly* heavy," Caroline Bradbury explained, as Klarinda returned to the front counter. "It weighs at least fifty pounds," she added in a half-whisper, as if she were filling Klarinda in on something top secret. Then she gave her Louis Vuitton mini steamer trunk a shove with the pointed toe of her high heeled pumps, and sighed theatrically.

"I'll bring it right up for you. You'll be in room number one. The yellow room right at the top of the stairs."

"Yellow? I hate yellow."

"I can switch you to a different room, ma'am. How do you like purple?"

"Don't call me ma'am. I'm younger than you are! The yellow room is fine. What difference does it make? It's just one night. But yellow's an ugly, unsettling color, if you ask me."

I didn't ask you, Klarinda thought. "I assure you, it's a pretty room," she said, smiling through her irritation.

"So," Caroline said, a little less caustically, "what have you got planned for me? Some kind of spa treatment or something? A massage?"

"What have I got *planned* for you? Well," said Klarinda, trying to hide how perplexed she felt, "there's Sand and Stone Spa on Fourth Street. That's a nice place. The Peabody sisters own it. In fact, I happen to have a brochure right here." She located one beneath her counter and handed it to Caroline.

"I'd have to *leave* this inn to get there?" asked Caroline, wrinkling her nose.

"Well, yes. It's probably about half a mile from here. Right down the mountain, then a few blocks down Main Street. And then you'd take a right on Fourth Street."

"Out there, in the snow?"

"Yes," said Klarinda. "You'd go through the snow to get there, of course. It's not as if there's a tunnel from here to the spa."

"I'd freeze to death," Caroline declared.

"There are a couple taxis around town. I mean, if Bob Harrison and Norm Richards are working today, anyhow. And one or the other usually is." She scratched her head, wondering if she'd answered this bizarre customer's question.

"Two taxis. That run when they feel like it. Charming."

"I apologize," said Klarinda, "but we're just a small town."

"Is this all some kind of joke? Am I in hell?" asked Caroline Bradbury.

"No. You're in Windy Pines," said Klarinda.

"I'm not impressed so far."

"Sorry to disappoint you," said Klarinda. She sighed. "Moving on, our dining room is open from seven to nine for breakfast, eleven thirty to one thirty for lunch, and five thirty to eight thirty for dinner. Here's a little card with the hours on it, in case you forget."

"Am I the only guest in this whole place?" asked Caroline, shoving the card from Klarinda into her handbag. She craned her neck, looking down the hall at the dark, empty dining room, and behind her at the dim, still parlor.

"For now, but we have other guests booked for this evening. It should liven up around here in no time!"

"That's a relief," said Caroline.

"One more thing, if you don't mind," said Klarinda. "We ask all our guests this: How did you hear about Mistletoe Manor?"

"What do you mean, 'How did I *hear* about it?'" asked Caroline Bradbury. Her eyes narrowed menacingly as she leaned over the counter toward Klarinda. "*You* invited me here."

"Excuse me?" asked Klarinda. "I'm pretty sure I didn't." She laughed a nervous, snorty little chuckle, and then hated herself for sounding like such a ninny in front of this woman. "How could I have, ma'am, when I've never met you?"

"Quit calling me that! Your boss must have invited me."

"I don't have a boss," said Klarinda. "I'm the owner of Mistletoe Manor."

"Enough of this silliness! I don't like it when people play games with me. If you didn't invite me, then explain this," said Caroline, pulling an embossed envelope from her handbag and setting it on the counter of the front desk.

Klarinda slid the card out of the envelope and opened it, and read the short message inside:

Dearest Caroline,

You're cordially invited to an evening of extravagance and luxury at Mistletoe Manor in scenic Windy Pines, Idaho.

Please use the airline ticket and taxi voucher included. All meals and expenses have been paid for. The evening of December 13 is reserved in your honor.

Don't miss this very special evening, or you'll certainly regret it. It will be a life changing evening!

Enjoy your stay!

Sincerely,

Your friends at Mistletoe Manor

Klarinda examined the card and the envelope. No return address, but it was postmarked Windy Pines. A plain white card with a raised MM on the front. It wasn't a card she'd ever seen associated with the inn. The envelope was equally simple and elegant, and made of the same heavy stock. She made a quick note of Caroline Bradbury's address: 171 North Salem St., Clear Water, New York.

"Is this *not* from you?" asked Caroline.

"I've never seen anything like it before in my life," said Klarinda. "Furthermore, no one paid for anything." She handed the invitation back to Caroline, just as the front door swung open.

"Brrr! It's freezing out," said the cute brunette who was stepping through the front door. She stomped off her boots onto the mat, and appeared to be just about to say something else, when her eyes met Caroline's and both women gasped.

"Caroline Bradbury?" squealed the brunette. "From Mount Hemlock Academy?"

"Tessa Wycliffe? Is that you?"

"It is! Me. In the flesh. Wow, Caroline Bradbury, my old roomie! Wild! It's been years! What are *you* doing here?"

"I was just asking myself that!" snorted Caroline.

"If you know one thing about me, you know that I'm a hugger! So you get over here," said Tessa.

14

Klarinda watched as Caroline awkwardly stepped forward and accepted Tessa's enthusiastic embrace. In Tessa's gloved hand was an envelope, exactly like the one Caroline was holding.

Chapter 3

Moments after Tessa and Caroline had checked into their rooms right across the hall from each other, the front door of the inn opened again.

"It's a brisk one out there," Todd Healy, the lone Windy Pines bike messenger announced. He was covered in snow and his teeth were chattering.

"How's it going today?" asked Klarinda, filling a mug with hot coffee from the machine behind her, and passing it to him. She'd had a crush on him since the first time he'd stopped by the inn two years earlier, delivering a 'Welcome to Town!' box of salted caramels from the folks down at the Windy Pines Candy Kitchen.

"Thanks for the coffee, Klarinda. I think by this evening I'll be hanging up the bike for the season and having to use my Jeep. I just about wiped out coming up here."

"Myrtle's about to plow our driveway. You can stick around here for a little while until she gets to it, if you'd like, so your trip back down isn't so bad."

"I'd love to, but I've got a few more deliveries to make, and I want to be done before the storm hits. Take care," Todd said, setting his nearly-full mug back on the counter along with the bulky manila envelope that he'd pedaled up the mountain to bring to her.

"You, too," she told him, and then added, "Stay warm out there," as the door closed after him.

Dejected, Klarinda tore the envelope open and reached inside. Her hand closed around the instantly recognizable papery-linen texture of cash. Thinking she must be imagining things, she peeked inside. Her eyes met a huge bundle of bills. She froze, looking all around her at the empty first floor of the inn. She could hear Pierre back in the kitchen, slamming pots and pans around, but otherwise, she was alone. She pulled the wad of bills from the envelope and set it on the counter. She began quickly flipping through the stack of hundreds and counting, and ended on an even one hundred. On the very last bill was a sticky note reading *This ought to cover it.*

Her heart seemed to have moved up a few inches, its drumbeat reverberating through her entire chest and neck. She looked around, waiting for Todd to return and say, "Gotcha!" or for Myrtle or Pierre to jump out along with a hidden camera crew. But the inn was calm and silent, and nothing unusual was happening.

She walked over to the front door and peered out the old nine-paned window. Aside from the rapidly falling snow and low, gray clouds settling over the inn, all was still. Todd Healy was gone, the tracks his bike had left already getting buried under fresh flakes of snow. The clock on the wall by the stairs was ticking the loud, deliberate seconds it always produced when she listened for them. In the far distance she heard a plow coming up the hill, and little else.

She shoved all ten thousand dollars back into the envelope and slid it beneath the counter, and immediately dialed Todd's number, which, mainly due to having too much time on her hands in a boring little town, she knew by heart.

"Hello?" he answered. She could hear the wind howling in the background.

"Hi, Todd. It's me. Klarinda Snow."

"Oh, hey. Did I forget something up there at the inn?" he asked.

"No. I'm wondering about this package you just delivered. Who's it from?"

"There wasn't any identification on it?"

"No. None," said Klarinda.

"Nothing identifying inside?"

"Not a thing."

"Well... Yikes! Chunk of ice in the road!"

"Be careful," said Klarinda, picturing Todd's cute, slightly weathered face.

"That package was left at my shop and the form was only partially filled out. Whoever left it just filled in the part about taking it to Mistletoe Manor, and they left me the five dollar delivery charge in cash."

"Strange," said Klarinda.

"It happens more than you'd think. People are half-assed about things," said Todd.

"Luckily you're not," said Klarinda, taking another look at the envelope's contents.

"Anything good inside? Never mind. It's none of my business."

"So there's no way for you to find out who left it?"

"Oh, shit! I just got splashed with a heap of slush. I think that asshole did it on purpose! I've got to get home before I freeze to death. Sorry I can't help you, Klarinda," said Todd.

"It's okay. Bye, Todd," she said, but he had already hung up.

Chapter 4

"Hi?"

"Am I hearing things?" Klarinda asked herself. She looked into the parlor, but it was deserted.

"Hi?" again came the call of a... person?

Klarinda crossed the parlor and looked into the dark dining room. She could just barely decipher the silhouette of a frumpy little woman standing alone in the middle of the room.

"I'm here to spend the night," said the woman.

"I didn't see you arrive," said Klarinda, setting down the pile of laundry she'd just retrieved from the basement. She squinted into the dark dining room. The woman was gripping the back of a chair.

"I got here a few minutes ago, but no one was around, so I took a little tour on my own. I hope that's okay."

"Oh, sure. Of course it is. Why don't you come up to the front counter and I'll get you checked in."

"It would be nice if you had fires burning in the fireplaces. It would feel more welcoming," said the woman, not budging from her place in the dark dining room.

"Good idea! We'll get those fires going any minute."

"Good," said the woman. "I pictured this place with fires burning. And where's your Christmas tree? There's at least one Christmas tree here, right?"

"Uhh," said Klarinda.

"*Tell* me there's a Christmas tree! A place that calls itself Mistletoe Manor owes its guests a Christmas tree or two. Or three. Or four."

"We're just one big disappointment, I guess," Klarinda muttered under her breath.

"What did you say?" asked the woman.

"The dining room is actually closed right now. Would you like to join me at the front counter? I'll get you checked in and show you to your room," said Klarinda. "This way." She walked through the dining room and back toward the front hall of the inn, hoping this guest would follow her.

"Okay," said the woman, slowly shuffling along. Now illuminated by the flickering sconces on the wall of the inn's main floor hallway, Klarinda saw that she wasn't nearly as old as she'd seemed.

"Do you have luggage along?" Klarinda asked her.

"Just this backpack. I'm only staying for one night." The woman set the backpack on the floor and placed her small, childlike hands on the front desk.

"Could I see your credit card and driver's license, please?" asked Klarinda.

"I don't drive, and I don't have any credit cards."

"Oh," said Klarinda. "Well, what's your name, please?"

"Benjamina McKellar. I go by Benji. I know what you're thinking. Like the dog, right?"

"I wasn't thinking anything," said Klarinda. "Here you are on my schedule. I've got you in the orange room." *And it suits you perfectly*, Klarinda noted to herself, seeing as how Benji's hair, freckles, shirt, pants, and sneakers were all varying shades of rusty orange.

20

"Is my room just up these stairs, here?" asked Benji, making no effort to pay for her room.

"Yes. Room number five. And, let me guess. You got a plain white invitation saying your room had already been paid for?"

"That's right. Good thing I enter so many contests! Thanks for picking me."

"No problem," said Klarinda, with a shrug.

She'd just begun folding the dishtowels in the laundry basket when the door swung open again and a man and a woman stepped through it, dusting snow off their shoulders. Klarinda watched as the airport shuttle haphazardly turned around in the driveway. Myrtle had plowed their driveway and parking lot twice now, but there was already another inch or two of snow on the ground.

"Welcome to Mistletoe Manor," said Klarinda. "You must be the Newcastles?"

"Actually, we just met at the airport, and shared a cab when we discovered we were both headed here," said the man. "I'm Jacob Reese. Here for one night." He shook the snow from his wavy dark hair and flashed a sexy smile Klarinda's way. She felt her cheeks get hot.

"And I'm Sara Byers," said the tall, rather plain woman. "Also here for one night."

"Sara and I compared notes on the car ride here, and it seems we've both won the same all-expenses-paid mini vacation," said Jacob. He pulled a plain white envelope from his coat pocket, for Klarinda to see.

"But, of course," she said weakly.

"Is this some kind of marketing gimmick?" asked Sara. "Not that I'm complaining. I needed a break from my four kids. They're all under the age of five. Yes, it's every bit as exhausting as it sounds! Since the twins were born, I haven't gotten a good night's sleep once this whole past year. It's just about more than I can take."

"It sounds rough," said Klarinda. "Jacob, you'll be in room three. It's the green room. Sara, you'll be in room six, which is our purple room." *I hope Myrtle got that damned toilet fixed!* Klarinda prayed silently. "Do either of you need some help with your luggage?"

"I've got it all," Jacob said, picking up his bag and Sara's bag with a chivalrous sweep of his arm.

You certainly do, Klarinda thought.

As they ascended the stairs, the front door of the inn swung open again, and an attractive blonde haired man with glasses and a black ski jacket stepped inside. "Am I okay to park right there?" he asked, pointing to a green Subaru resting crookedly beside the dumpster corral.

"Yes, that's fine," said Klarinda.

"Great. Sorry about the parking job. Best I could do, with the conditions out there."

"You're fine," said Klarinda. *Yes, you are!* she added silently.

"My name's Christopher Murdock. I've got a reservation for the night. I almost didn't make it, though. They're closing the road between here and Elk's Pass. I'm hoping I can get out of here in the morning. If not, I guess you'll have me for two nights."

"They're closing the road?" asked Klarinda.

"That's what they said on the radio." Christopher unzipped the duffle bag he was carrying and reached inside, pulling out a now-familiar white invitation. "Do you need this?"

Klarinda sighed. "No, you keep it."

"Is this because I'm a 94.7 preferred listener?"

Klarinda just shrugged.

"Anyway," said Christopher, "thanks for covering airfare and taxi fare, but I live just an hour and forty-five minutes from here, up in Coldwater City. I figured it was easier and faster to drive."

"Oh. Okay," said Klarinda. She handed him his room key. "Room number four. The gray room. At the top of the stairs, you'll go straight down the hall and to your left, across from room number three."

"So, can I redeem my airline ticket and taxi fare voucher for some other trip?"

"I've got to confess," said Klarinda. "You all seem to be part of a mystery, and I'm afraid I'm not in on it."

"What do you mean?" asked Christopher.

"Just what I said."

"You still haven't answered my question."

"Take it up with the airline." She passed him a card with the dining room hours on it.

"Thanks," he said, shoving the card in his pocket. "So," he said, leaning in flirtatiously, "this isn't *your* place, right? You're too young for that. Right? Are you the manager, or do they call you the front desk girl?"

"Nope. This is my inn. I own it. Just little ol' me. Anything else I can help you with?"

"I guess not," he said, sighing and heading up the stairs, leaving Klarinda to her dishtowels, confusion, and throbbing temples.

"The dining room's open for business in five minutes," said Chef Pierre, a few minutes later, turning on its lights.

"I'll get the fire going," said Myrtle, who was just stepping through the front door. She was covered in snow and grease. "That doggone plow," she said, in explanation for her disheveled appearance. She was followed by Kelsie Bantam, a local high school student who served as one of the inn's only two waitresses.

"Sorry I'm late," said Kelsie. "Driving here was really scary."

"I understand," said Klarinda. "It might be busy tonight. The inn is booked and I wouldn't be surprised if some folks from town venture out, too. Should I call Addie to come and help out?”

“I kind of want the tips,” said Kelsie. “But, yeah, maybe you ought to call her. I can only do so much.”

Klarinda had just finished leaving messages on the other waitress’s cellphone and home answering machine when the inn’s front door swung open again and a scowling woman entered. Her pant legs were soaked from the knees down.

“My goodness,” exclaimed Klarinda, setting down the phone. “You must be freezing!”

“That’s putting it mildly,” said the woman. She tossed her butter yellow hair back away from her round, pretty face. “The taxi driver dropped me off at the bottom of the hill since he couldn’t even decipher where your driveway was.”

“Has *that* much snow come down since Myrtle last plowed?” asked Klarinda.

“I can’t tell you when *Myrtle* last *plowed*,” said the woman, putting the name ‘Myrtle’ and the word ‘plowed’ in air quotes, “but if I’d been able to stay on the driveway when I walked up here, it probably wouldn’t have been so bad. However, it’s *so* poorly lit out there that I stumbled into a snow bank! Can you *please* get me checked in so I can take a hot shower and change out of these frigid clothes?”

“Of course. What’s your name, please?”

“Alanna Newcastle. I go by Lannie. Here you go,” she said, whipping out her ID and handing it to Klarinda. “The reservation is probably under my husband’s name: Tom Newcastle. He was going to come along, but something came up at the last minute. Like it always does.”

“Thank you,” said Klarinda, taking Lannie’s license.

“And this little cutie-muffin is Pumpernickel. She’s my little Yorkie-poo,” said Lannie, patting the head of the fluffy creature tucked under her arm in a quilted pouch. Then she began speaking in babytalk to the dog: "Aren't you a cutie-muffin, Pumpernickel? Who's a little Yorkie-poo? Did Mommy keep you all warmy-warm-warm and toasty-toasty-roasty in your widdle carrying bag? No big, bad snowstorm for you!"

"I'm sorry," said Klarinda, "but we don't allow pets."

"Are you *kidding* me?" yelled Lannie. "This is a service dog! Tell me 'no' again and I'll sue you."

Klarinda sighed. "I didn't realize it was a service dog. In that case, yes, your dog is welcome here."

"That's more like it!" said Lannie.

"You're in our Rose Suite. It's the red room at the top of the stairs. Room number seven. It's our only suite, and if I do say so myself, our nicest room. The dining room is right down the hallway, and dinner is being served from now until eight thirty tonight. Here's a card with the breakfast and lunch hours as well. Do you need help with your bag?"

"No," Lannie said, shaking her head and disappearing up the stairs.

"Sorry about the driveway," Myrtle whispered, popping out from the basement as soon as Lannie was gone. "We're going to have to get a mechanic over here. Something's wrong with the plow. I'm afraid it's going to fall right off the truck. It's dragging on the ground. I can't even drive that truck the way things are right now."

"Let's get Phil the Plow Guy over here. We can't have the driveway blocked off like this," said Klarinda.

"Good idea. I'll give him a call," said Myrtle. She glanced up the stairs, and then whispered, "So, did you learn any more about what brought our guests here?"

"No, except that the first two knew each other."

"Oh. Well, that makes a little more sense," said Myrtle.

"Only, they were surprised to see each other. They hadn't intentionally booked their stay here to be together. In fact, they both looked shocked to see one another."

"What kind of a wacky coincidence is that?" asked Myrtle.

"I know! Right?" said Klarinda. "This whole situation is baffling. They've got these fancy, embossed invitations that I've never seen before, telling them that they've won a night's stay here. And Myrtle, get this: Their airfare and taxi rides here, all the way from the airport, were even covered! They all assume I know what it means, and that I'm the one who invited them, or that they won some kind of contest or something. But I haven't got the foggiest idea what's going on. Did anything like this ever happen when the old owners were here? Some kind of murder mystery party, or something like that?"

"Not that I recall," said Myrtle. "And trust me: I wouldn't forget something like that, because this place isn't exactly known for its exciting times."

"That's what I was afraid you were going to say," said Klarinda. "I ought to add, it's a tough crowd. They're the biggest bunch of weirdos and snots I've ever dealt with."

"It might be the bad weather getting to them," said Myrtle.

"Maybe that's it. The other thing is that they all seem to be pretty young. I've got photocopies of most of their drivers' licenses and they're all between the ages of twenty-six and twenty-eight. Rather unlikely, wouldn't you say? Our average visitors are middle-aged couples."

"Maybe this is becoming a singles' hotspot," said Myrtle. Her eyes lit up at the thought of it.

"Ha! Why am I still alone then?" asked Klarinda.

"I hear ya," sighed Myrtle. "Do you think Pierre's ever going to warm up to me?"

"I think Pierre will only ever truly love his copper pans," said Klarinda.

"Yeah, I suppose an old bag like me can't compete with something that new and shiny," said Myrtle.

Klarinda laughed. "Maybe Phil the Plow Guy has some room in his heart. I heard Martha left him?"

"He's not my type," said Myrtle. "I just can't date a man who's shorter than me."

"Despite being height-challenged, he's a cutie," said Klarinda.

"Did you hear who Martha left him for?"

"Please, please don't tell me that she left him for my secret boyfriend Todd the bike messenger."

"I wasn't going to," laughed Myrtle. "She left him for the high school principal."

"The Windy Pines school principal? That old geezer with the walking stick? No way!" exclaimed Klarinda.

"So, you like that Todd Healy, do you? You know, I went to school with his mother," Myrtle said, nodding thoughtfully. "She had him really young. We were seniors in high school."

"Put in a good word for me the next time you see her," said Klarinda.

"Ex*cuse* me," said Caroline Bradbury. She and Tessa Wycliffe were standing at the bottom of the stairs. Klarinda and Myrtle had been so caught up in their gossiping that they hadn't even heard the women approaching. "Anybody home?" Caroline sneered, stomping up and hitting the small bell on Klarinda's front counter four times in a row. "I hate to interrupt your hen-talk, ladies, but this little card you gave me says that it's dinner time." Caroline waved the card in their faces.

"Oops. Sorry," said Klarinda, doing a one eighty from happy to stunned in just under two seconds.

"You *should* be," said Caroline. "We were standing there for I don't know how long, waiting for someone to help us, and you both just *kept* ignoring us! Seriously, I can't wait to give this place a terrible review."

"Don't mind my old friend," giggled Tessa. "She's a little mouthy when she drinks." Tessa made a move to tuck her own mini bottle of vodka into her purse, but it fell to the floor. "Oopsie daisy," she said, stumbling to pick it up.

"Yes, the dining room is open. Follow me," said Klarinda, doing her best to remedy the situation while Myrtle went off to call the snow plow guy. "Would you ladies like to be by the fireplace or the windows?"

"Considering how cold it is in here, you'd better put us by the fireplace," said Caroline.

"Certainly," said Klarinda, through a clenched smile, relieved that Myrtle had actually gotten the fires going. As she turned away and Kelsie stopped over at their table with a pitcher of water, Jacob Reese made his way into the dining room. He'd clearly been napping, by the look of his wrinkled shirt and bedhead. If possible, this look was even hotter. Klarinda caught her breath, and involuntarily sighed a little sigh of appreciation.

"Hello, Jacob," she said. "Could I seat you over here by the window?"

"Sure," he started to say, but then he, Tessa, and Caroline all spotted one another at the same moment.

"What the heck? No way! No freakin' way! Is that *you*, Jacob Reese?" shouted Tessa.

"Is this some kind of Mount Hemlock Academy reunion?" asked Caroline, flaring her nostrils and looking around suspiciously.

"Tessa," said Jacob, somewhat brightly. "Caroline," he added, gravely.

"Join us at our table," said Tessa, pulling out the chair from a nearby table and shoving it between herself and Caroline, and then patting it enthusiastically half a dozen times.

Jacob hesitated.

"Pretty, pretty please," whined Tessa.

"Are you okay with this?" Jacob asked Caroline.

"Sure," she said, barely looking at him. "You can sit anyplace you'd like in this whole stupid dining room. Why should *I* care where you sit?"

"Okay," Jacob said, sitting down between Tessa and Caroline.

"Would you three like a larger table?" asked Klarinda, since the one they were squeezed around was really meant for just two.

"Yes," said Tessa. "We'll take this one." She plunked her purse and water glass down on the large table behind them and sighed. "This is all so strange. The three of us together here. What are the odds of all of us winning the same contest?"

"Not very good," said Caroline. She glared in Klarinda's direction, still assuming that someone from Mistletoe Manor was behind all of this. Not wanting to get interrogated about it, Klarinda slinked out of the dining room, despite her overwhelming desire to stay and eavesdrop.

When she stepped back out into the front hallway, Sara and Lannie were both waiting for her at the front desk.

"I think she was here first," Sara announced, nodding over at Lannie.

"Hi, again," said Lannie, waving from the corner.

"Oh, yes. The woman with the service dog," said Klarinda. "How may I help you?"

"I'll stay right here, if you don't mind," said Lannie, who was dressed in a bathrobe, trying to hide behind the coat rack by the front door.

"Okay, but if the door opens, you're going to get knocked over," Klarinda warned her.

"Fine," Lannie said, taking a few steps toward the front counter. "I'll stand up here in plain view, but let's make this conversation quick! Somehow, probably because my husband makes my life *so* hard, I forgot to bring shampoo and conditioner. I figured I'd soldier through since it's just one night. I figured I could use whatever you've supplied – you know, kind of go with the whole 'I'm camping' mentality," she said, using her beloved air quotes. "But there's not *any* shampoo or conditioner in my shower. I'm half frozen from that hideous walk up here, and I *need* to take a hot shower *now* before I catch a cold."

"I'm afraid we don't supply the rooms with any toiletries other than soap," said Klarinda.

"Are you joking? What kind of a luxurious inn is this?" she cried, her fingers weakly scratching around 'luxurious inn' as tears welled up in her eyes.

"You can borrow some of my shampoo and conditioner," Sara said to Lannie.

"Thanks, but you don't need to do that," Lannie said to Sara, and the two women locked eyes for the first time. A cloud of recognition passed over Lannie's face.

"Hey! I *know* you. I mean, you look really familiar."

"You do, too," said Sara.

"Did we go to grade school together?" asked Lannie.

"Maybe. Are you from Indianapolis?" asked Sara.

"No," said Lannie. "I grew up in Miami. Did you happen to go to boarding school?"

"Yes!" said Sara.

"I *knew* I knew you! Are you Sara Johnson from Mount Hemlock Academy?"

"I used to be Sara Johnson. I'm Sara Byers since I got married six years ago. I'm sorry I can't remember your name, but I definitely remember you now."

"I'm Lannie Newcastle. You probably remember me as Alanna Winthorpe. I was a couple of grades below

30

you. You were our floor's 'big sister' when I was a sophomore. In the Carvington Dorm."

"Oh, yes. I remember you now." Sara drew in a deep breath, her face turning white. "How could I have forgotten you? You were Avery Burtz's roommate."

"Yes. Yes, I was," said Lannie.

There was a long moment of awkward silence.

"Do you ever hear from Avery's parents?" asked Sara.

Lannie shook her head. "No. Not for years, anyway."

"It was such a tragedy. You must still be haunted by it," said Sara.

"No," said Lannie, her voice barely audible. "I mean, yes. I mean, I try not to think about it much. It was so long ago. I've tried to put it behind me."

The two women stood frozen for a couple more awkward moments, before Klarinda decided it was proper to break back into the conversation.

"How may I help you?" she asked Sara.

"Something's the matter with my toilet."

"Oh, dear," said Klarinda. "Let me track down Myrtle. She'll get it fixed for you in just a moment."

Sara sighed and she and Lannie exchanged a look that said they both were used to much nicer accommodations than what Mistletoe Manor was providing for them. Klarinda pretended not to notice.

"We have communal restrooms down that hallway, for you to use until Myrtle gets around to fixing your toilet," she said to Sara. "I'm so sorry about the inconvenience. And," she added, reaching beneath the counter for her emergency supply, "here's a travel sized shampoo and conditioner for you, Lannie. It turns out we did have a couple of spares."

Chapter 5

"We're going to have to get a plumber out here," Myrtle said to Klarinda. "I've tried everything I know and I can't get this blasted thing to work."

"It figures. Why is it so hard to get ahead in life?" Klarinda lamented.

Myrtle laughed. "You crack me up, girlie. I'll call Rod Showers. His rates are reasonable. And he's a hottie!"

"Myrtle, are you serious? He's got to be seventy years old," said Klarinda.

"Easier to catch him," said Myrtle, wiggling her eyebrows. She picked up the front desk phone, but Klarinda set it back down.

"That can wait for a second. Are you ready for this?"

"Ready for what?" asked Myrtle.

"The plot thickens! They all know each other from boarding school."

"They do?"

Klarinda nodded. "The five of them having dinner, anyway."

"Hmmph," said Myrtle. "I see they're all sitting together at the same table. Good thing you never got ahold of Addie. There wouldn't have been enough work to go around tonight." Myrtle lowered her glasses, then raised them back up, and then lowered them again. "Am I *seeing* things? Why's that little blonde haired one wearing a bathrobe?"

"Because she was going to take a shower, until she decided to go warm up by the fireplace," said Klarinda, rolling her eyes, "and by then they'd all realized they knew each other from some fancy schmancy boarding school they all went to. Some of them didn't realize it at first, like that super cute guy Jacob, and the tall, plain woman, Sara, but now they've all figured out their connection, and they've been in there getting drunk together ever since."

"This is turning out to be a very peculiar evening," said Myrtle, picking up the phone.

"You don't know the half of it! Apparently Lannie, the one in the bathrobe, had a roommate who died, or something. I'm not really sure, but it sounded sinister. And I haven't even told you about the envelope Todd delivered," Klarinda continued, but then she trailed off, wondering whether she really wanted to talk about it. Her gut told her that receiving so much money in an unmarked envelope was bad news. But her brain was spending it faster than her gut could keep up.

"You know, I recently prayed for something exciting to happen around here," Myrtle remarked. "I guess my prayers have been answered."

The sound of heavy footsteps on the stairs made Klarinda and Myrtle look up. Benji McKellar was making her way down to them, still dressed in her wrinkled, rusty orange outfit, her hair a snarled nest piled on top of her head. Christopher Murdock was a few steps behind her, now dressed in jeans and a long sleeved t-shirt with a picture of a woolly mammoth on it.

"Is the dining room right through there?" Christopher asked Klarinda and Myrtle, nodding toward the open doorway down the hall.

"That's right," said Klarinda. "I'll show you to a table."

"I'm here to eat, too," said Benji.

"Great! Follow me," said Klarinda. She fully expected these two to turn out to be part of the Mount Hemlock Alumni as well, so she wasn't surprised to hear the entire table begin shouting things like, "Hell, no! Is that you, Murdock?" and "Chris freakin' Murdock. No *way*, man!"

Naturally, Christopher Murdock found himself a place at the table.

"Are those your friends, too?" Klarinda asked Benji. The young woman stood back hesitantly, seeming to be overwhelmed by the raucous good time happening at the table in front of them. Then she shook her head.

"I'm not with them. You can just seat me wherever," she said.

"Do you want this table by the window? It's a little quieter over here," said Klarinda.

"Sure. This is fine," she said, glumly.

"Kelsie will be your waitress. She'll be right over with some water," she said, leaving Benji with a menu.

On her way out of the dining room, as Klarinda passed by the large table holding the rest of the guests, she couldn't help but notice that Caroline's chilliness toward Jacob had passed. She was running her hand down his arm and laughing at something he'd just said. They were all gloating about the Ivy League colleges they'd attended and how successful they ended up being, except for Christopher, who was getting good-naturedly picked on for having only attended some state school.

"You mind staying up here for a bit?" Klarinda said to Myrtle, when she returned to the front counter where Myrtle was waiting on hold for the plumber to answer the phone. "It's time for turndown service," she added.

"Go right ahead. I'll be here anyway," said Myrtle. Klarinda scooped up a handful of mints and an armful of toilet paper, and made her way upstairs with the master key to make her nightly rounds.

She started with Alanna's room, the red suite at the top of the stairs. Wet clothes were discarded in a sloppy heap on the bathroom floor. A small piece of high-end luggage was parked beside the bed, still primly zipped shut since she'd gone straight for the inn-supplied robe. Pumpernickel was fast asleep in the center of the bed, behaving herself much better than her mother. This room had its own little kitchen in it. Klarinda noticed a water glass and open bottle of anti-anxiety medication sitting beside the sink.

She switched on the lamp, turned down the covers of the bed, but skipped the mint, erring on the side of keeping the dog from getting sick.

Next up was the small hallway with the blue and yellow rooms. Tessa's room was room number two, the blue room. As soon as she opened the door, Klarinda was overwhelmed with the stench of alcohol and cigarettes. She marched over to the window, despite the blizzard going on outside, and opened it as wide as it would go. "Do you know how hard it is to get the smell of cigarettes out of curtains, rugs, mattresses," she muttered under her breath. The inn had a strict No Smoking policy that was clearly advertised on its website, not to mention the No Smoking sign on the door, and the table toppers on the desk, bathroom counter top, and bedside table. Yet there were people who still didn't listen. She shook her head in disgust, flipped back the covers, and tossed a mint on Tessa's pillow. "I hope she chokes on it," she added.

Next up was Caroline Bradbury's room. The yellow room. "*I* think yellow's pretty," Klarinda said to herself, stepping around the Louis Vuitton trunk. It was shocking how quickly this room had gotten trashed. Clothes were all over the bed, the sink was full of strands of blonde hair and globs of lotion and toothpaste, and the television was blaring. The room smelled heavily of perfume. The ceiling fan was going, and a curling iron had been left plugged in, half an inch away from the drapes. Klarinda unplugged it and set it in a safer location. "Good thing I have insurance, with guests like these," she whispered.

Somehow Caroline had managed to use up nearly an entire roll of toilet paper already. Klarinda left her a spare roll, and went to flip back the bed covers, when she noticed the white envelope resting on the bedside table, sticking out from a fashion magazine. She went over and picked it up, and pulled the card from the envelope. Unfortunately, there were no clear identifying marks indicating where it had come from. She sniffed it and was surprised to discover it smelled kind of musty. Like a basement.

She put it back where she'd found it, deposited the mint onto the pillow, and moved on to room number four, the green room. Home for the night of the gorgeous Mr. Jacob Reese.

He hadn't settled in at all yet. The room was tidy and looked exactly the same as it had looked before he'd arrived, with the exception of a small wrinkly dent on one side of the bed where he must have rested before dinner. The room smelled faintly of some kind of sexy men's cologne. Klarinda sucked in a long, deep breath of it, just as she noticed his invitation sticking out from his open jacket pocket. She tiptoed over to the door and peeked out the peephole, making sure she was still alone up here. Then she grabbed the invitation and took a quick look. It was exactly like Caroline's. She sniffed it. Musty smell and all. She put it back where she'd found it, took one last look, and moved on.

Across from Jacob's room was the gray room where Christopher Murdock's was staying. He'd certainly made himself comfortable. The closet was filled with his clothes and shoes, and the glass by the bathroom sink held his toothbrush and toothpaste. Sensing that she was taking too much time, and possibly crossing over into a slightly creepy territory she prided herself on not venturing into (a tricky row to hoe, as an innkeeper), Klarinda picked up her pace. She deposited a mint on Christopher's pillow, and was about to pop into Benji's room when Rod Showers, the plumber, appeared at the top of the stairs with Myrtle right behind him.

"I hear you've got some toilet trouble," he announced.

"Yes. Thanks for coming over so late, Rod. And in this storm! I should have called you weeks ago, but we don't use that room very often, so it's easy to let these things go. Right down this hallway," said Klarinda, leading the way.

"You're busy. I'll stay with him," Myrtle whispered, shooing Klarinda away.

"He's all yours," Klarinda whispered back.

She returned to Benji's room. It was neat and orderly, and looked pretty much exactly as it had looked before she'd arrived. Klarinda always found it interesting how some people truly settled in and lived in their room, even if only for one night, while others preferred to live out of their suitcases.

"What's *your* story?" Klarinda whispered, looking around for some kind of clue. How had this little frumpster wound up mixed in (or should she say, left out) with this mix of rich, spoiled, prep school alumni? She had told Klarinda that she'd also received an invitation, but why would she have, if she wasn't part of their group?

Klarinda stuck her head out into the hallway and listened. Myrtle and the plumber were chattering away in the purple room's bathroom. Otherwise, the second floor seemed to be empty, with no sign of Benji or anyone else.

Klarinda clicked the door shut and darted over to Benji's backpack. She was about to unzip it when she heard the sounds of the doorknob rattling, and a key scraping into the lock. She shot straight up and was flipping the covers back and placing a mint on the pillow when the door swung open.

"What are you doing in here?" snapped Benji, looking shocked.

"Just getting your room ready for the night," said Klarinda.

"Oh. You scared me. I didn't know anyone would be in here."

"Sorry. I'm about to get out of your way. Did you have a good dinner?"

"I guess it was alright. The gravy was lumpy. In my head, I pictured it smooth."

"I'll talk to the chef," Klarinda said, even though she had no intention of mentioning the complaint to Pierre.

"Good," said Benji. "I wasn't expecting you to care."

"I care," said Klarinda, feeling immediately guilty.

"Another thing," said Benji, "is that there are typos in your menu."

"There are?" asked Klarinda.

"Yes. Beef bourguignon is not spelled b-o-u-r-g-u-i-n-i-o-n," she said.

"Okay. Sorry about that," said Klarinda.

"And there should be a space between ice and cream in ice cream. Obviously."

"Well, yeah. I guess I noticed that one already, but it costs quite a bit to get them reprinted. Anyway, thanks for pointing that out."

"I went to Harvard. Not that you'd have to go to Harvard to be able to spell ice cream."

"Good for you," said Klarinda.

"I'm not trying to brag. It's just that I heard that stuck-up group of pretties going on and on about how they went to Princeton and Yale and Oxford. But none of them went to Harvard."

"Pretties?" asked Klarinda.

"That's what I call pretty people. People like that group sitting around the table. They're nothing. Just a bunch of pretties."

Klarinda wasn't sure why she felt compelled to continue carrying on with this conversation, but she'd never been one to hold her tongue when she felt she ought to speak up. "I don't know if it's fair to hold someone's success against them. And really, I don't think a lot about where people went to college. I'm in my thirties, and at this point, it doesn't mean that much to me. Honestly, it never has."

"You're just saying that because you must not have gone anyplace good. Back to what I was saying, you ought to get your menus fixed."

"I heard you the first time. Anything else you need? Otherwise, have a good night," said Klarinda.

"I suppose you think I'm arrogant, but I'm just trying to help you improve. I wish someone had helped me improve at some point in my life, but I've always been on my own."

"Maybe I have, too," Klarinda said. "You shouldn't assume things about people."

Benji snorted a little at that. "You can, though. Statistics can explain quite a bit about most situations. Back to helping you improve, though. A better menu would add to the experience of staying here. And a Christmas tree. It's deplorable that there isn't one. You're setting people up for disappointment. I'm trying to help you. So far, this experience hasn't been the best."

Klarinda nodded. "Okay. Sorry you feel that way. I'll leave you to your privacy now…" she said.

Benji yawned and sat down on the edge of the bed, and continued talking, ignoring Klarinda's cue. "It was getting busy down there. I figured I'd had enough. I don't like that much noise!"

"Well, the dining room closes at eight thirty, and we stop serving alcohol at ten thirty, so you won't need to worry about it going on all night. Do you need any extra towels or anything like that before I go?" Klarinda asked, her hand on the door frame and one foot out the door.

"No. You mean they're going to be down there until ten thirty?"

"Well, actually, it could be a little later. We stay open until eleven, but last call is at ten thirty. Honestly, though, you won't be bothered by them. These old walls are thick. Even if the dining room is busy until eleven, it doesn't usually affect the people who are upstairs."

"It affects me," said Benji.

"Okay? Well, my work is done here. Have a great night," said Klarinda. She had the door half closed, but then she paused and stuck her head back in Benji's room. "Quick question for you, if you don't mind my asking: What made you decide to stay here at Mistletoe Manor? We like to know these things. For marketing purposes."

"Like I already *told* you," said Benji. "I got invited. By you, I thought. I got an invitation telling me I won a free night's stay."

Klarinda nodded. "That's right. I forgot. Did you have to travel far? Do you still live in Massachusetts?"

"I'm surprised you know that's where Harvard is. You'd be surprised how many people don't even know that much."

"So, is that where you're from?" Klarinda tried again.

"Could you please excuse me? I have a terrible headache," said Benji, lying back on the bed, closing her eyes, and rolling over to face the wall.

"Of course," said Klarinda. "I hope you're feeling better."

"I will be soon," said Benji. "You can close the door after yourself. Goodbye."

Chapter 6

"I've never seen so many people here," Kelsie said to Klarinda.

"You're doing a great job. I'll get this table by the doorway. Just do your best," Klarinda told her, before heading over to the four elderly gentlemen in reindeer sweaters. They were rather famous around town for traveling about on skis and caroling all winter long, fearlessly facing whatever weather Windy Pines had to throw at them.

The clock on the wall said it was eight fifteen, but people were still piling in, and the inn's policy was to serve dinner to anyone who appeared before eight thirty. *Poor Pierre*, thought Klarinda. He must be pulling his hair out back there, alone in the kitchen.

Klarinda approached the old men's table to take their order, since Kelsie was barely keeping up.

"Just some eggnog and a big basket of fries for us," said the old man who most resembled Santa Claus.

"Bless your hearts. Your order will be right up," said Klarinda.

"Do you mind if we do a little caroling while we wait?" asked the one with the droopy mustache.

"That would be wonderful. You go right ahead," she said, before rushing over to greet a couple who looked like they were in their teens.

"We snowshoed here," the boy announced, his cheeks red from the gusting wind.

"School's been canceled for tomorrow, so we decided to celebrate," added his girlfriend. Then the cute couple looked at each other adoringly.

Klarinda nodded, trying not to admit to herself that she was jealous of a couple of sixteen year olds. She showed them to one of the last remaining tables in the dining room.

Just then some activity happening in the parlor caught her attention.

"Can I help you?" she asked the two men in khaki coveralls who were setting a Christmas tree stand in front of the old bay window.

"Is this a good place for it?" asked one of them.

"It would be if I'd ordered a Christmas tree," said Klarinda.

"You didn't?" asked the other.

"Nope."

"Isn't this Mistletoe Manor?" asked the taller guy, consulting his worklist.

"It certainly is, but I never ordered a Christmas tree," said Klarinda.

"Oh. Well, someone from here called in an order for our budget-friendly Douglas fir with white twinkling lights and sixty childproof burgundy ornaments. They also checked the box for a burgundy felt tree skirt and the small assortment of wrapped empty packages to set beneath it. It says here... someone named Myrtle ordered it. Are you Myrtle?"

"Just set it up," said Klarinda, too frazzled to argue.

She hurried back to the dining room, just in time to see the old men stand up and begin their barbershop quartet style show of caroling. The room hushed and time stopped for a moment, giving Klarinda a chance to focus on her overnight guests at the big table again.

To her irrational disappointment, Jacob and Caroline were still all over each other. Tessa and Christopher were also getting cozy, and Lannie and Sara were huddled together, deep in conversation. Lannie was still wearing the bathrobe, despite that there were six tables of other diners surrounding them.

"Isn't this great?" Myrtle asked, sneaking up behind Klarinda. "This is why I love living in a small town. By the way, the toilet's fixed, it only cost forty dollars, and Rod Showers gave me his personal phone number. He's only sixty-two, by the way!"

"How lucky can you get?" whispered Klarinda. "So, you went ahead and ordered us a tree?"

Myrtle shrugged. "I had to do what I had to do. Are you mad?"

"Nah. It was probably the right move. As one of our guests said, a place called Mistletoe Manor really does need to have a Christmas tree."

Myrtle nodded. "True," she said.

"By the way, this is the worst group we've ever had at one time. I don't know what I'd do if I didn't have you to vent to."

"Has that woman seriously eaten her whole dinner while wearing only a bathrobe?" asked Myrtle.

Klarinda nodded. "Classy establishment we've got here."

Just then Lannie seemed to realize how ridiculous she looked, and she rose from the table. Hugging the wall the whole way, she edged herself around the room like she was clinging to the side of a building, then raced up the stairs to her room.

"Smooth," Klarinda whispered to Myrtle, both of them smirking.

Sara then seemed to realize she was a fifth wheel, so she set some money on the table and also headed upstairs.

The barbershop reindeer sweater oldies wrapped up their act and the dining room erupted into good-natured applause.

"Not to be outdone," announced Christopher Murdock, untangling himself from Tessa, "I've got a little holiday ditty for you. Let me get a beat rolling on my phone," he said. He smoothed his *Don't be a bully, be a woolly!* t-shirt and cleared his throat.

"You're such a doofus," Tessa giggled drunkenly.

Seconds later a peppy little beatbox rhythm filled the room and Christopher broke out into a song about snow angels and candy canes that he seemed to be making up as he went along. The other diners, instead of being annoyed or irritated by these little shows, ate them right up. They caught right on to Christopher's song, and before long the whole room was singing along.

"I'm up next," said Jacob, trying to outdo his old friend with a rap about wrapping paper, but failing miserably. He sat back down when he was done and took a big swallow of beer.

"Shake it off," said Caroline, giving him a little hug.

"Let me!" shouted an older woman in the corner, jumping up as soon as Jacob had sat back down. Much to her embarrassed husband's dismay, she belted out *Silent Night*, and was met with much applause.

"This is turning out to be quite the great evening," said Myrtle, her eyes shining.

"I couldn't agree more. When I bought this inn, I imagined us having nights like this. Fun, spontaneous, special times," said Klarinda, just as the festivities were derailed by an ear-piercing scream.

Chapter 7

"I just wanted to get a little shampoo and conditioner from her. The kind you gave me was so cheap. I couldn't bear to use it," said Lannie.

She was still in the robe, leaning over Sara's lifeless body, her face pale with shock. Klarinda and Myrtle, and nearly all the diners who'd moments earlier been enjoying themselves, were gathered around, or waiting in the upstairs hallway, on the stairs, or in the downstairs hallway. "Please, someone call 911," Klarinda yelled to the crowd behind her.

"It's too late for 911. She doesn't have a pulse," Lannie sobbed. "I already checked."

"We still need to call 911," said Klarinda. "Did you find her right there, halfway in her bathroom and halfway out?"

"Yes," said Lannie, nodding emphatically. "I knocked on her door and she didn't answer. I waited a little while, and I even considered showering with the samples you gave me, but I couldn't do it. This color costs a fortune. Those samples would probably turn it all brassy and dry, and give me split ends. So, I knocked again, and she still didn't answer. I thought it was kind of strange, so I tried her door and that's when I discovered her lying here...

dead!" Lannie burst into tears, burying her face in her hands.

"This has got to be particularly difficult for *you*," said Caroline Bradbury, who, thanks to being a head taller than most of the people around her, had a good view of the scene.

"No kidding," said Tessa, shaking her head in disgust.

"What are you two getting at?" asked Klarinda.

"Never mind them," said Christopher. "They're both drunk."

"Would everyone up here please go back downstairs?" Klarinda said to the crowd. "There's no need for you to all gather up here. Has anyone called 911 yet? And please don't forget to settle your bills and tip your waitress before you leave."

"Oh my goodness," wailed Lannie. "Would you look at that? There's pink foam on the corner of her mouth. She's been poisoned!"

"I mean it," Klarinda yelled. "Everyone, get out of here. You too, Lannie. Myrtle, would you please call 911 in case no one else has yet?"

"I called them already. They should be here any second, if they can make it through this blizzard," said a voice from the hallway.

It was Benji. She waved her hand in the air. "I called them," she repeated. "I just got off the phone with them. Help is on the way."

"Thank you," said Klarinda. There was a smattering of applause, which struck Klarinda as ironic, considering ten minutes earlier they'd all been clapping for carolers.

Just then the sound of sirens cut through the noise, and people began clearing out to make way for the first responders.

Chapter 8

"What a night," said Klarinda, an hour and a half later, when she, Pierre, and Myrtle were cleaning up the kitchen together.

"It's tragic," said Pierre, shaking his head.

"At least we closed early," said Myrtle, glancing at the clock on the wall. It was just quarter to eleven.

"I wouldn't have minded staying open," said Klarinda, since she seemed to be the only one who ever remembered that they were running a business.

"What do they think happened to her?" asked Pierre.

"When they heard there had just been a plumber here, the police figured it had something to do with the hydrochloric acid he used to clear the drain line," said Klarinda. "Maybe she inhaled it, or got some on her toothbrush, or something like that. I think they were on their way to talk with Rod Showers."

"Oh no! I hope Rod's not in trouble," said Myrtle.

Klarinda shook her head. "I don't think they suspect foul play. Still, the sheriff should be back in town tomorrow morning, weather permitting, and the police who were here tonight said he'll stop in to talk with us more. They said he's visiting his sick mother up in Elk's Pass tonight, and the road's closed. So who knows what will happen next."

"If he's busy they could send over Deputy Franklin," Myrtle suggested, naming the hot new officer about town.

"That would be nice," Klarinda agreed. "From the sound of it, the police really have their hands full this evening. They said there have been several accidents, and that the avalanche warnings for north of town are on high alert."

"So Deputy Franklin's busy with real emergencies? Darn it!" Myrtle joked.

"No kidding," said Klarinda. "How do we get a 'real emergency' to take place here?"

"You two," said Pierre, shaking his head. "The police force must be feeling a little overwhelmed. There's not often much happening around here."

"I'll bet you're right. Did you see we were voted the safest community in all of Idaho?" asked Klarinda, referring to an article she'd read in the *Post Register* the previous month.

"Aha! You're starting to become a local," said Myrtle.

"What do you mean by that?" asked Klarinda.

"You're getting proud of your town," said Myrtle. "I told you it would happen! Didn't I tell you, when you first moved out here and you were homesick, that one day you'd wake up and Windy Pines would be part of you? And that you'd never be able to leave!"

"I guess I am starting to think of Windy Pines as *my* town," mused Klarinda, picking up a dirty pan.

"I'll take care of that," Pierre added, taking his beloved copper pan from Klarinda's hands.

"Oh, that's right. These are your babies," she said.

"So I love my pans. So what?"

"No judgement here," laughed Klarinda. She took a swig from the open bottle of brandy they were sharing and passed it to Myrtle. Sipping from a bottle of brandy and sharing a bag of chips while they did the dishes had become the Mistletoe Manor crew's nightly tradition.

"Don't mind if I do," Myrtle said to Klarinda, taking the bottle from her. "So, can I ask you something?" she said.

"Sure. Ask away."

"How old are you?"

"You *know* how old I am, Myrtle! Anyway, don't you know that you're never supposed to ask a woman her age?"

"That's only true if the woman is older than you," said Myrtle.

"Maybe I'm older than you," said Klarinda.

Pierre reached for the bottle and took a swig. "This is getting good," he said.

"I'm thirty-four," said Klarinda. "I'll be thirty-five in March. How old are *you*?"

"I'm fifty-three," said Myrtle. "Now, back to you, how'd you end up owning this place, all alone? I know for a fact that when the Petermans sold this place they were asking over half a million dollars for it. How'd you come up with all that money? And why would a young, single gal like yourself want to take on all this responsibility? I've been meaning to ask you this for two years!"

"What stopped you?" asked Klarinda.

"Oh, I don't know. I suppose since it's none of my business."

"We're friends now," said Klarinda, "so it is too your business." She took the bottle from Pierre. "I wound up here because I thought it would be relaxing and picturesque." She took another swig. "I paid for it with money I'd earned over ten years in the advertising industry.

I used to live in Chicago. I used to have to wear suits and high heels every day! Can you picture it?"

"No," Myrtle and Pierre said in unison.

"I wanted a change of pace, and I really thought I had what it took to turn this place around." She took another swig. "And the biggest reason I wanted it? Well, I thought it would be a guy-magnet."

At that Myrtle and Pierre both burst into laughter.

Their laughter was abruptly cut short, however, by the sound of a crash upstairs.

"What the hell was that?" exclaimed Pierre.

The three of them darted out of the kitchen, through the hall and up the stairs, and then paused in the upstairs hallway between Lannie's suite and the guys' rooms, trying to determine where the sound had come from.

"Hello? Is everyone okay?" called Klarinda to the closed doors before her.

"What *was* that?" asked Benji opening her door and scowling out at them. She looked half awake. Klarinda noted that even her pajamas were that same shade of rusty orange.

Caroline's door opened then and she and Jacob stepped out, both wrapped in sheets and blankets. They joined the others in the larger portion of the hallway. "What's happening now?" asked Jacob.

"That's what we're here to find out," said Klarinda. She began knocking on each door.

"I'll get the master key. Just in case," said Myrtle, dashing down the stairs.

One by one the doors opened. Lannie's door, and Christopher's a moment later, until five of the six remaining guests were standing in the hallway. Klarinda went over to Tessa's door and rapped on it as hard as she could.

"Tessa? Are you in there? Please come out! We're worried about you," shouted Klarinda.

"Here's the master key," hollered Myrtle, barreling up the stairs. She tossed it to Klarinda, who then opened Tessa's door in a hurry.

"Aarghh!" screamed Klarinda, jumping back. Everyone came rushing forward to get a better look.

"Oh, no! No! Not again," yelled Lannie, clutching Pumpernickel to her chest. She and the little dog were dressed in matching pink nighties. Klarinda tore her eyes from that spectacle to the bigger problem: The ancient, solid oak armoire that had always been a focal point of the blue room had somehow toppled over, and Tessa was crushed beneath it, lying in a pool of her own blood. A tiny bottle of vodka lay beside her open hand, making its own little puddle.

"How could this have happened?" asked Klarinda. "That armoire weighs hundreds of pounds and is just about impossible to move! How in the world did she manage to knock it over on herself?"

"Let me check for a pulse," said Pierre, rushing in and raising Tessa's limp wrist. They all waited in nervous anticipation. After several long moments he shook his head and solemnly placed her hand back on the floor.

"It's all our fault. This happened because she was going after her vodka and cigarettes," said Caroline.

Jacob stepped forward, hanging his head. "We put them up there so she'd stop smoking and drinking, and just go to bed."

"We thought we were helping her," said Caroline.

"You two drunks were trying to help her," scoffed Lannie. "I mean, no offense. I'm just saying."

"But she must have climbed up there to get them, and then pulled the armoire down on herself," Jacob continued, as if Lannie hadn't even spoken.

"But do you think she's going to be okay?" asked Benji, straining her neck, trying to get a better look.

"She's not okay! She's dead!" said Klarinda.

"I guess I ought to call 911 again?" asked Myrtle.

Klarinda nodded. "Thank you, Myrtle," she said, forcing herself to look away from the horror.

"I'm going to get back to cleaning the kitchen," said Pierre, skulking off.

"If she would've come to my room like I asked her to, she'd still be alive right now," Christopher noted.

Klarinda stood up, doing her best to gain control over the situation. "Alright, everyone. Please, go back to your rooms. The police will be here soon. This has clearly been a terrible accident. There's nothing any of us can do."

"Are we going to leave her lying there? In her own blood?" exclaimed Lannie.

"The least we could do is pick up the armoire," suggested Christopher.

"I suppose you're right," said Klarinda.

"Let me help," said Jacob, tying his bedsheet into place and stepping forward. Klarinda would have preferred him not to, seeing as how lifting the armoire was going to mean also dragging her new, five hundred thread count sheets in the blood. But mentioning such a thing seemed crass and heartless, so she bit her lip instead.

"On the count of one... two... three," said Christopher. He and Jacob lifted the armoire, tilting it back until it settled heavily in its original place.

"Ugh! I wish you guys hadn't done that," said Lannie. She blocked Pumpernickel's eyes with her hand.

"Cover her with a blanket, please," said Caroline. "She looks like a squashed squirrel you'd see on the street."

"Here. Take mine," said Benji, bringing in the $250 duvet that Klarinda had just purchased a few weeks earlier. Before she could argue, the duvet was covering Tessa.

"Alright, everyone," said Klarinda. "Please go back to your rooms. The police will be here again soon, I'm sure, but unless they need to speak with any of you individually, I'm going to ask you to stay in your rooms. And I don't normally say this to guests, but in light of everything that has happened tonight, I'll be downstairs in my apartment if anyone needs me throughout the night. Good night."

Chapter 9

The clock beside Klarinda's bed said 1:17 when she sat up in bed, wide awake. She listened, trying to figure out what had woken her up. The inn was quiet and nothing seemed out of sorts. The police had left about thirty minutes earlier, and she'd fallen asleep minutes after she'd locked up after them.

Now she was as alert as a jackrabbit, but she had no idea why. She got up and peered out the window. The snow was still coming down. The bottom half of her window was covered; she had to stand on the ottoman to look outside. An old hanging lantern cast a shallow yellow glow across the parking lot of the inn. It highlighted the snowflakes and Christopher's crookedly parked Subaru, and not much else.

Klarinda crawled back into bed and was just dozing off again when she heard what she guessed to be the sound that had woken her in the first place: Somewhere in the inn, a woman was crying.

She got out of bed, opened the door from her apartment to the back hallway of the inn, and listened. Now she could hear it more clearly. She followed the sound, up the stairs, and straight to Lannie's room. The wailing coming from inside was growing louder and louder. She saw a sliver of light appear beneath Caroline's door, and realized that Lannie was waking up the entire inn, so she knocked lightly on her door.

"Hey! Are you okay in there?" she called, when the wailing continued.

The crying stopped and the door opened a crack.

"Sorry," sniffled Lannie. "Was I that loud?"

"No, no. Not at all," Klarinda lied. "Clearly, it's been a very strange, upsetting evening. Is there anything I can do to help?"

"I don't know. Maybe I just need someone to talk to," Lannie said. "Death always makes me really sad," she added through her tears.

"I think that's pretty normal," said Klarinda.

"Come in. Sit down," said Lannie, gesturing toward the small living room of the suite.

"Sure," said Klarinda, closing the door behind her and taking a seat in the paisley wingback chair.

Lannie placed her dog on Klarinda's lap. "Please, comfort her. I just... can't," she said. Then she flung herself on the love seat and picked up a crumpled tissue from the coffee table and loudly blew her nose into it. After several honks, she buried her face in a pillow, snotting it up like nobody's business. Just when Klarinda was considering whether she ought to get up and leave, Lannie shot back up, ready to unload.

"When I was back at the academy, something horrible happened," she said. "Do you already know about this? I mean, I suppose someone else has already filled you in on all the sordid details."

"Actually, no," said Klarinda. "I don't know anything about what happened at the academy."

"I want to tell you, but I'm afraid you're going to j-j-judge me," Lannie bawled.

"I won't judge you," Klarinda promised.

"Good! Because I really need to get this off my chest!"

"Go ahead," said Klarinda, "but if you wouldn't mind keeping it down a little..."

"Right," said Lannie, lowering her voice a smidge. "So, it was my sophomore year, and I was about to turn sixteen. The crazy part is, the night I'm talking about was ten years ago *exactly*. It was a Wednesday night. It's almost like *this* reunion has something to do with *that*. I don't know?" She shrugged helplessly.

"Go on," said Klarinda.

"I had decided to have a sweet sixteen party, and I'd been planning it for weeks, and it was going to go on for days. From December thirteenth through December seventeenth."

"That's quite the celebration," said Klarinda.

"I guess," said Lannie. "My actual birthday is December sixteenth, so I had this idea like I might as well celebrate all weekend. Since I didn't live with my parents, I had to throw the party for myself. That sounds kind of strange, I guess, but everyone at the academy did that. Sweet sixteen parties were a huge deal, and it was normal to plan your own, and you know, just have your parents send you the money to pay for it. And it was normal for them to last several days. You can relate, right?"

"Oh, sure," said Klarinda, thinking back to her own impoverished childhood, growing up in the tiny town of Orfordville, Wisconsin, and being raised by her disabled grandparents.

"So, I planned an amazing party for myself, because my mom and dad said that the sky was the limit. I bought myself a bunch of outfits, because I was going to do several costume changes, just like everybody else had done at their parties, and I even got my parents to buy me a car."

"Your parents bought you a car," Klarinda repeated, "as part of a birthday party?" *I was lucky to get a piñata,* she added in her head.

"Well, yes and no," said Lannie. "I was turning sixteen anyway, and they knew I'd need a car, so even though I hadn't passed my driving test yet, they called a local dealership, bought me what I wanted, and had it delivered to the academy. You know, with a bow on it and all of that. Like lots of kids' parents did."

"Wow," said Klarinda, looking around the room, making sure she hadn't slipped into some parallel but very different universe.

"Anyway," Lannie continued, "I invited everyone who was anyone. I didn't have a boyfriend, so I invited, like, every cute boy in the whole academy. I invited plenty of girls too, so I didn't look like I was totally boy-crazy. Tessa and Caroline were roommates, right across the hall from me, so I invited them. I invited their boyfriends, Christopher and Jacob. Honestly, I invited anyone who was even remotely cool, because I'm an inclusive person. I always have been. I hate hurting people's feelings. But I didn't invite my roommate Avery. I just couldn't. She was too gross. I hated her! She would have ruined my party."

"How would she have ruined it?" asked Klarinda.

"Everything about her was all wrong. And keep in mind, I was sixteen. Things are harder at that age. And kind of magnified, you know?"

"That's true," said Klarinda.

"Sure, during the summers we got to be home, or vacationing, or whatever, but during the school year, being trapped together in that teensy room... So many hours together, non-stop. Ugh! She drove me nuts!" Lannie shuddered in ick-filled remembrance.

"I can imagine," said Klarinda.

"She had really bad skin that she picked at. And she picked her nose right in front of people! She was really unhealthy. She ate fries and candy bars for every meal! Her clothes were hideous. She got terrible grades. There were even rumors that she was going to get kicked out of Mount

Hemlock, since she was on a scholarship and wasn't doing well enough to stay. You understand why I didn't invite her, right?"

Klarinda didn't like where this was going. "So, what happened to her?"

"Like I said, it was a Wednesday night, and I'd just gotten back from the mall with some new shoes. I went straight to Tessa and Caroline's room to show them. They were hanging out with Christopher and Jacob, watching some movie. They loved my shoes! I sat down and started watching the movie, too. It was... Oh, shit! I mean, sorry for swearing, but I just remembered what it was. It was *Mean Girls*, of all things. Ugh! I'm making it sound like we were a bunch of bullies, but we weren't. Really! Being not interested in someone doesn't make you a bully."

"Okay," said Klarinda, since Lannie seemed to be waiting for some feedback. "Were you guys *ever* nice to her? Did you *ever* include her in anything?"

"See, there you go. Getting judgy," said Lannie. "I knew I should have kept my mouth shut."

"Forget I asked," said Klarinda.

"We weren't bad to her," Lannie insisted, tears filling her eyes again. "Christopher, for instance, used to stick up for her. She probably never even knew that. Anyway, the door to Tessa and Caroline's room was open, so Sara stuck her head in to see how we were doing. She was our floor's big sister. That's like an upperclassman hall monitor, kind of. Just for the record, she was *so* much cuter back then. I didn't even recognize her when I first saw her again. Having ten kids certainly didn't do her any favors! Just saying. Gosh, I sound horrible, don't I? Speaking ill of the dead like this."

"You mean to tell me that ten years ago tonight, the six of you who were just sitting around that table were all together, watching a movie?" asked Klarinda.

Lannie nodded. "And once it was over, I went back across the hall to my own room. And that's when I discovered Avery."

"Discovered Avery..." Klarinda repeated.

Lannie nodded. "Yes," she said. "I discovered her. Lying there. Dead." Her voice cracked on the word *dead*.

"That's terrible," said Klarinda. "What happened?"

"I screamed! *That's* what happened! Tessa and Caroline, and Christopher and Jacob, and Sara... Well, they all rushed over, trying to calm me down. I was *so* upset!"

"I meant, what happened to Avery?"

"Oh, yeah. Avery. She had swallowed an entire bottle of sleeping pills, and left me a note that said '*This is all because of you, Alanna. Thanks for inviting me to your party. Not!*' Can you believe she *did* that? I've never, ever forgiven her! As you can imagine, it was the worst night of my life."

Klarinda nodded. "I'll bet."

Lannie yawned. "Oh my gosh! It's three in the morning! I've got to get some sleep! Thanks for listening."

"Anytime," Klarinda said, handing Pumpernickel over to Lannie and letting herself out.

Chapter 10

At four twenty-three, Klarinda awoke to a strange sensation. She was so tired that at first she tried to convince herself it was a dream. *So I'm being rained on*, she told herself. *No big deal. It's a warm rain, and a little rain never hurt anyone.*

But it didn't stop, and it was too real, and suddenly she knew it wasn't a dream at all.

She sat up in bed, and wiped at her wet face. She reached behind her, patting at her pillow, and discovered that the entire side of her pillow was damp. She was about to reach for her lamp, but even in her groggy state, she thought better of it. Instead, she got out of bed, walked across the room, and turned on the lamp by her doorway instead. To her horror, the plaster ceiling above her bed was dark, damp, and dripping water. She did a quick mental calculation, realizing that she was directly below the yellow room's bathroom. Without further hesitation, she grabbed the master key and sprinted up the stairs to Caroline Bradbury's room.

She knocked loudly on the door, not caring who she woke up. By the looks of that spot on her ceiling, the entire bathroom must be flooded, and she'd be lucky if the old seventy-two inch clawfoot bathtub didn't come busting right through the second floor down onto her bed!

When there was no answer, she let herself into the room. The bed was empty, and it was a rumpled mess. Wine bottles were spilled on the floor, and an open bottle of whiskey sat on the bedside table. A black lace bra dangled from the lampshade and a bottle of massage oil lay in the middle of a dark, greasy stain on the bed. The bathroom door was closed, but the crack under the door showed that the light was on inside.

Klarinda didn't have time to feel bad about having yet another set of ruined sheets. She ran over to the bathroom door and pounded on it. "Hello? Are you okay in there?" The carpet here was squishy and soggy. When no one answered, she turned the knob and swung open the door. Water was everywhere. It was flowing over the center, dipping edge of the tub, flooding the entire bathroom. And in the tub – Klarinda rubbed her eyes, almost not believing what she saw -- were two lifeless bodies floating face down.

Klarinda leaned into the small bathroom and turned off the gushing faucets. She didn't have to flip the bodies over to know they were Caroline Bradbury and Jacob Reese.

Chapter 11

"I'm starting to think we should set up camp here," Deputy Franklin joked grimly.

"That might not be a bad idea," Klarinda agreed, setting a tray with hot cups of coffee in front of him and the other officers.

"I've got to admit," said one of the officers who'd already been out to the inn earlier in the evening, "I can see how *one* person could drown in a bathtub, but two at one time? That's got to be a one in a million kind of thing."

"No kidding," said his partner, who had just finished up interviewing Pierre, Myrtle, and the remaining guests, despite that all of them had been asleep when it happened.

"Do you mind if you and I sit down for a more in-depth interview? It's Klarinda, right?" said Deputy Franklin, his blue eyes piercing inquisitively into her own eyes.

"Yes, Klarinda. I mean, yes, my name is Klarinda. And no, I don't mind. Being interviewed. By you," Klarinda stammered. *You sound like an idiot*, she screamed silently at herself. *And a guilty idiot at that!*

Despite that they'd already had two other tragedies at the inn earlier in the evening, this was Deputy Franklin's first visit to Mistletoe Manor. He'd been preoccupied with five car accidents of minor and major proportion, the looming threat of avalanches, and a burglary that had turned out to actually be a lack of communication, when a husband had told his neighbors they could stop by and borrow a box of Christmas lights from the garage, but he'd forgotten to mention the plan to his wife. At least these had been the excuses the other officers had given as to why the handsome deputy was an hour later than them getting to the inn, and why he hadn't shown up previously.

Klarinda recalled having seen Deputy Franklin's face in the local paper when he moved to Windy Pines back in the fall. Since then she'd seen him around town several times, and once up close and personal at the Windy Pines Natural Foods Cooperative, but she hadn't spoken to him before. She had, however, already decided that if things never came around with Todd Healy, she wouldn't mind getting to know the single deputy a little better. Unfortunately, now was her big chance, but instead of sparks flying and the two of them exchanging witty banter, she was a bumbling, fumbling mess. Her lack of sleep and having a semi-destroyed inn weren't helping her state of mind.

"Should we sit down in here?" Klarinda asked, leading him to the parlor at the front of the inn.

"This looks good," he said, closing the double pocket doors after them. "Do you mind if I record our conversation?"

At this, Klarinda stiffened a little. "I don't mind. But, I'm not in any trouble, am I?"

"No. Not at all," said Deputy Franklin. "I just don't want to miss anything important."

"Okay, then. I guess it's fine," she said. It didn't *feel* fine, though. She immediately began thinking of every bad thing she'd ever done. Was she going to get in trouble for photocopying people's credit cards? There were endless incriminating paper copies in her to-be-shredded pile. Did he know that she'd gotten an underage drinking ticket in high school? And what about that envelope of money? She swallowed. She supposed she'd better say something about that money.

"Relax," Deputy Franklin said, laughing. He reached out and squeezed her wrist for one electrifying second. "You're not in trouble. I realize this has been a chaotic, exhausting, and very sad night."

"It has," said Klarinda, nodding. "...been all three of those things."

"And, as unlikely as it is, Coroner Birkus doesn't suspect foul play in any of the four deaths."

"Four deaths," Klarinda repeated. "Here at Mistletoe Manor." She rubbed her forehead. "I just realized that no one's ever going to want to stay here again. People are going to think this place is cursed!"

"I'm sure they won't," said Deputy Franklin. "Are you up for answering a few questions?"

"Yes," said Klarinda. "Please go ahead."

"Okay. Let's focus on the drowning of guests Caroline Bradbury and Jacob Reese. When did you last see either of them alive?"

"I saw them both when Tessa was killed by the falling armoire, just before eleven o'clock. They explained how they'd set her alcohol and cigarettes up on top of it, to keep them away from her, and that she must have crawled up there to get them. Then the officers showed up, and they were talking to Jacob and Caroline for a while. I guess that's the last time I saw them."

"Wait a minute," said Deputy Franklin. "*Those* two were trying to keep Tessa from drinking? I find that rather ironic. There are at least four empty bottles of wine in their room."

"Not to mention the whiskey," Klarinda added.

"That was the last time they were seen, though?" asked the deputy.

"Yes. ...But, wait! I just remembered that later I heard Lannie crying, so I got up to try to quiet her down, and at that time I noticed that she'd woken up Caroline and Jacob. I saw the light come on beneath Caroline's door when I was standing in the hallway talking to Lannie. So, I didn't actually *see* them, but they were in there, awake at that time. The lights were on, anyway."

"What time was that?"

"I forget," said Klarinda. "A little after one o'clock, I think."

"Okay. Let's talk about when you found them."

Klarinda nodded, wincing a little.

"Sorry. I can't imagine how difficult this is for you."

"Thank you," said Klarinda.

"Do you recall whether the door to their room was locked?" he asked her.

"It was. Well, then again, I'm not sure. You see, as soon as I saw the ceiling above my bed, I knew we were in big trouble. I grabbed a master key, and ran up there, and knocked on the door. When no one answered it, I used the key to let myself in. It's possible it was unlocked already, but once you stick the key in the lock, turn it, and push the door open, you'd never know if it had been locked or not."

"Most visitors lock their doors, though. Right?" asked Deputy Franklin.

"Usually, but most of these guests know each other, so they might not have."

"They know each other?" asked Deputy Franklin, looking interested.

"Yes. All the guests but one went to the same boarding school. It was called... let me think... Mount Hemlock Academy."

"All but one of them?"

"That's right," said Klarinda.

"And which guest is the one who didn't go to that school?"

"The one named Benji," said Klarinda, feeling a little as though she was throwing the orange haired girl under the bus.

"Would you mind getting him for me?" asked Deputy Franklin.

"Not at all," said Klarinda. "But for the record, Benji's a her."

"Oh. Okay. That works."

"I'll be right back with her."

Chapter 12

"I can't believe my rotten luck. If I don't make my flight, I'll miss Tom's holiday work party," Lannie pouted. "And *then* what will happen?"

"I'm not sure," said Klarinda. "Would you like to set down your water glass for a moment so I can top it off?"

Lannie ignored Klarinda, flailing her glass around to punctuate her complaining. "Well, let me *tell* you what'll happen: He'll probably get drunk in front of his boss, and throw himself at Geraldine Johnson, just like he did at last year's holiday party, only this time I won't be there to stop him. And then what?"

"I really don't know."

"Well, let me tell you: He'll probably get his sorry ass fired! This horrid trip to Mistletoe Manor, the inn from hell, is going to cost my husband his job. With me here and him there, that means a hundred percent of his common sense isn't even in the same state as his penis. I should have known better than to come here."

"You're right about that," said Benji, sliding her glass over to Klarinda.

"Not to mention, it's almost my birthday," Lannie continued. "I swear, if I'm still stuck here, in these 'luxury accommodations' on my birthday, I might keel over and die. I mean, not die. I guess that was the wrong thing to say. I'm just saying, I'm *so over* this terrible trip."

Klarinda nodded. "I do feel your pain, Lannie. Trust me. I do. But all roads in and out of Windy Pines are closed, so I don't think you're going to make that flight. So, for the last time, would you like that refill of water?"

"Did you add lemons to it like I requested?" Lannie asked, eking out a snivelly little smile.

"Yes," said Klarinda.

"Sure. I guess it's the least you can do," Lannie said, handing her glass to Klarinda.

Lannie, Benji, and Christopher were sitting at the big table in front of the fireplace, having some lunch. Myrtle had gotten a nice, crackling fire going, and Pierre had made a bigger effort than usual, fixing the three remaining guests a delicious lasagna lunch, but there was no satisfying them. Even Christopher, who hadn't stopped grazing from the complimentary bowls of peanuts and candy around the inn since he'd first arrived, had now lost his appetite. Seeing the two body bags getting carried out earlier in the day, coupled with being trapped in Windy Pines, seemed to be severely impacting the remaining surviving guests' moods.

"Would any of you care for dessert?" Klarinda tried.

All three guests shook their heads.

"Mercy me," Myrtle said, bustling through the dining room. "I've got fans and dehumidifiers working their magic up in the yellow room, and in your apartment, Klarinda, but I think the problem is even bigger than we thought. That wet spot on your ceiling has spread all the way to the corners!"

"Stay out of there," Klarinda warned. "Undoubtedly, there's going to be some structural damage. My main concern right now is keeping everyone who's still here safe!"

"I'll be careful," Myrtle assured her, disappearing into the kitchen.

"I'm going upstairs to take a nap," said Christopher, rising from his chair and exiting the dining room.

"I've had enough socializing, too," said Benji, a moment later, pushing her plate of lasagna away. She followed after Christopher.

"On second thought, I'll have some dessert," Lannie decided. "I might as well try to find a little bit of happiness in this sea of misery."

"I'll bring you a menu," said Klarinda.

"No, no. I'm too tired to make any decisions. Just bring me some cake. Any kind of cake. As long as it's fresh, of course. I mean, you guys *do* have cake, right?"

"Coming right up," said Klarinda.

A few moments later she returned to the dining room with an oversized slice of Pierre's famous chocolate vanilla marble cake. She'd taken a couple extra minutes to plate it beautifully, centering it on a squiggle of fudge sauce and covering it in white chocolate shavings, doing her best to cheer up her most impossible remaining visitor. But now the room was empty.

"Seriously?" she asked the empty room.

She began clearing the table with one hand, still holding the cake in the other, when Lannie returned, coming from the direction of the parlor, yawning.

"I just realized that there aren't any televisions down here! How do you function without TV?"

"We're trying to take people back to a better, more wholesome, more connected time," said Klarinda.

"Ha! That's actually funny."

"Would you like this piece of cake?"

"Naaa. I changed my mind. I don't need cake. I guess I might as well take a nap, too," said Lannie. "There's nothing else to do in this sorry place." She leaned over next to the chair she'd been seated in a moment earlier, to the quilted bag where Pumpernickel had been sleeping while she dined, and she screamed.

"What's the matter?" asked Klarinda, dropping both the cake and the armload of dishes she'd just cleared from the table.

"Pumpernickel is missing! She's been kidnapped! She's gone! Are you *listening* to me? Someone's stolen my little peanut butter cup!"

"Maybe she just hopped out of her carrying case and went exploring?" Klarinda suggested.

"Pumpernickel doesn't *explore*. She's a Yorkie-poo, not some scent trail crazed *hound* dog! My little Pumperbee sticks by my side!"

"Weren't you just in the parlor? Maybe she's in there."

"I would have heard her tapping along beside me."

"I'm sure she's around here someplace," said Klarinda. She bent down and began picking up the broken bits of plates and glasses. "As soon as I've taken care of this mess, I'll help you look for her."

"Thanks for nothing," Lannie muttered. She sighed, looped the little dog's pouch over her shoulder, and traipsed off to find her. "Here, Pumpernickel! Here little Pumpiepoo! Where's my little Pumpernickel? Who's a good girl?" she cooed, heading back to the parlor.

Klarinda took her time picking up the sharp chunks of glass and china. The last thing she needed was one more person getting hurt. Even a scratch would be bad, considering everything else that her guests had endured at the inn in the past sixteen or so hours. She'd just wiped up the last of the splattered lasagna and cake, and could still hear Lannie's obnoxious trill off in the distance imploring, "Will my teensy widdle baby pweese come out and see me?" and then, to Klarinda's relief, "*There* you are, Pumpiepoo!" when a deep, guttural, creaking grunt overtook the inn. It was like the rumbling in the belly of a hungry monster.

"What *was* that?" Klarinda whispered to herself.

It happened again, and this time it was followed by the sound of crashing, and breaking, and what sounded like water splashing. Klarinda didn't even know which way to run. The sound had seemed to come from every direction at once. At that moment, Pumpernickel came racing past, coming from the direction of the back hallway where the restrooms and Klarinda's apartment were. The little dog raced toward the parlor, and did a lap through the dining room, hall, and back through the parlor, before Klarinda's shock subsided and she sprang into action.

"Is everyone okay?" she yelled.

Myrtle and Pierre both came bursting into the dining room, through the swinging kitchen door. "What was that?" asked Pierre.

"I was getting some firewood from the pile out back, and Pierre was taking out the trash, but we heard it all the way out there," said Myrtle.

"I'm afraid to find out," Klarinda admitted. All three of them raced toward the stairs. Halfway up to the second floor they heard Benji and Christopher's simultaneous screams, and saw the two of them standing just to the right of the top of the stairs, in the hallway that led to the yellow room.

"What's going on?" asked Klarinda.

"The floor..." said Christopher, pointing and trailing off.

"Is gone," Benji added.

Myrtle, Pierre, and Klarinda came up behind Christopher and Benji, looking through the space between them into the doorway of the little yellow guestroom. Four or five fans whirred and a dehumidifier hummed, and beyond it all, the open door to the bathroom revealed... nothing. Absolutely nothing. No clawfoot tub. No antique wooden vanity. No porcelain toilet. No black and white tiled floor. The floor and everything that had rested on it were all, simply… gone.

"No!" Klarinda yelled, realizing what had happened. "Everyone, get downstairs, and get away from this part of the inn. Go to the parlor or the dining room. Stay on that side. Immediately!" And with that said, she raced back down the stairs and straight to her apartment, through its tiny living room, to her bedroom. And then she screamed. Of course everything from one floor up had to land somewhere, but it was still shocking to see it.

The toilet lay broken in half on the floor. The antique vanity lay busted in pieces beside the bigger chunk of the toilet. And the clawfoot tub… Klarinda drew in a deep breath, trying to wrap her head around what she was seeing.

The clawfoot tub had crushed her bed. And in the puddle of water, plaster, tiles, and debris, face down by the foot of the bed, lay Lannie, her blonde curls soaked in blood.

Chapter 13

"What I don't understand," Klarinda told the police officer, "is why there was water everywhere."

He nodded, dinging the little bell on her front counter. "That's loud! I like little bells like this. You don't see them much anymore."

"Thanks," she said, setting it beneath the counter. "Back to the accident…"

"Go on. I'm listening," he said, reaching in his pocket for a tiny notebook.

"When I say there was water everywhere, I mean *everywhere*," said Klarinda. "I'm talking about gallons and gallons of water."

"Hmm. Yep, I can picture it," he said. *WATER EVERYWHERE!?!?!?* he wrote in his little notepad.

"Of course you can picture it. I just *showed* you what I'm talking about."

"Yup," he said.

Klarinda sighed and stole a glance toward the front window. She was hoping to see Deputy Franklin or the sheriff arriving, but there was no sign of activity out in the Mistletoe Manor parking lot. Just more snow coming down. This officer standing before her was some new guy she hadn't seen yet, and he didn't look like he was even old enough to shave.

"I'm talking about the water everywhere in my bedroom, when the ceiling collapsed," she added, since, despite having seen the scene of the accident, he seemed so confused.

"Because it was a bathtub?" he asked, giving her a quizzical look.

"Yes, but it should have been empty. They drained it. I thought they did, anyway. We were worried about something like this happening. The weight of it all, and the inn being so old. It was built in the 1880's."

"Oh. Okay," said the officer. *1880's! STAGECOACH INN??!??* he scrawled on his page, trying to block his notes from Klarinda's prying eyes with his other hand.

"This was never a stagecoach inn. Not to my knowledge," she told him. He drew a line through what he'd just written. "But when I went into my bedroom," she continued, "and saw what had happened, the room was soaked. And not just from the water spraying everywhere from the pipe above."

"Hmm... Yep, interesting. Go on," he said. *WATER SPRAYING?!!* he wrote on his tablet. Then he whispered, "Would you quit looking at my notes, Miss Snow? These are private police business."

"Sorry. I'm just... It's just that I can see what you're writing and I want to be sure you're getting it right."

"Trust me. I'm the law," he said, his face turning red.

"Anyway," Klarinda continued, "as I was saying, the tub pretty much dropped straight down and since it landed on the bed, and... err..."

"And on the body," he said, helping her along.

"Yes," said Klarinda, "And the body. My point is, when the tub dropped, it didn't break, so I could plainly see that it was still half full of water. After that big drop! How could that have happened if it had been drained?"

"Calm down, Miss Snow," he said.

"All things considered, I'm calm," said Klarinda, liking him less and less. She was stroking Pumpernickel's furry little shoulders, trying to soothe the dog, who seemed able to sense the loss of her owner.

"Do you mind telling me what the victim was doing in your bedroom?" asked the officer.

"I guess she was leaning over my bed, or maybe crawling under it, trying to get at her dog."

"And that's the dog she was looking for when it happened?" asked the officer.

Klarinda nodded. "Yes. This is her dog. Pumpernickel."

"Pumpernickel?"

"Yes. The dog's name is Pumpernickel."

"Like the brandy?" asked the officer.

"Like the bread," said Klarinda.

"And why was the dog in your apartment? Had you taken a shine to it? Were you hiding it in there?"

"No!" Klarinda exclaimed. "The dog was nosing around, I suppose, and found its way in there."

"Interesting. Very interesting," said the officer.

"Will Deputy Franklin be here soon? Or the sheriff? Or any of the other officers who were here earlier? A lot has happened here. Maybe if all you officers could meet here and get on the same page?"

"There's only one page, Miss Snow, and it's the page with the facts."

"Okay?" said Klarinda.

"You're not the only excitement happening around Windy Pines. Or the county, for that matter. This whole corner of the state is smackdab in the middle of an emergency. Don't you know there's a blizzard going on?"

"I'm well aware of the blizzard," said Klarinda.

"Good," nodded the officer. "The sheriff can't get into town. The roads are all closed, in case you haven't heard. And Deputy Franklin, last I heard, was in the middle of delivering a baby up on Wolf Lookout Road."

"Must be Charlotte Wilkinson's daughter Nicole's baby," Myrtle remarked, stepping through the front door of the inn from her most recent bout of shoveling, just in time to hear this part of the conversation. Her eyes were wide and worried. "I hope everyone's okay. Delivering a baby in this blizzard? That's a scary thought!"

"I'm not at liberty to say whose baby it is," said the young officer. "But yeah, it's Nicole Pelzner's baby."

Klarinda nodded. "Back to the most recent accident here..."

The officer closed his little notebook and put it in his pocket. "You said they drained the bathtub. *Who* drained it?" he asked Klarinda.

"I'm not sure. Maybe one of your officers? Or the coroner, after he took away..." she paused, not wanting to say *the bodies.*

"Well, it could have been considered a crime scene, so maybe they didn't want to drain it. Maybe the officers who were out here earlier figured there was evidence in that bathtub."

"I thought the officers who were here earlier said that no foul play was suspected?" asked Myrtle, coming up behind the deputy. "So what do you mean by 'it *could* have been considered a crime scene'? If we're in the middle of a crime scene we have a right to know! We've been shoveling snow and making lunch and carrying on like it's business as usual!"

"I... I'm not sure," said the officer.

"Didn't anyone fill you in on what's been happening up here? Wouldn't you *know* if it was a crime scene? Should we be worried? We've had five 'accidents' here in one day!" Myrtle continued.

"Miss Snow, are you in charge here, or is this lady?" asked the officer, getting bristly.

"I own this inn," said Klarinda, "but I don't mind having Myrtle's involvement. She's a big part of this inn and this town, and she raises some good points."

"Excuse me for just a minute while I take care of some important, secret, official business," said the officer, stepping from the front hallway into the parlor. He tried to close the pocket doors after himself for a little privacy, but couldn't figure out how to get them out of the wall, so he gave up. A moment later they heard him requesting backup. "No, not *that* kind of backup," they heard him saying. "Sorry. I didn't mean to alarm anyone. I just meant... are there some other officers who can come out here, too?" And then in a whisper: "I think I might be in over my head."

"What's going on here?" Klarinda whispered to Myrtle. "And how'd this little twerp get put on our case?"

"I *know* they drained the tub," said Myrtle. "When I was putting the fans and dehumidifiers in the yellow room, I saw it. If it hadn't been empty I would have drained it myself! Even if that meant sticking my hand in that nasty water! There's no way I would have left the water in there! Not with those weak, soggy floorboards beneath it!"

"I just realized something," said Klarinda, scrunching up her face and gagging a little.

"What's that?" asked Myrtle.

"When I woke up with water dripping on me, it was water from their bathtub. With them in it. Ewww."

Myrtle nodded. "Yup," she said. "I wasn't going to mention it, in case you hadn't thought of it."

"Alright, ladies," said the officer, "I hear you gagging and crying, and I realize this is all very gross and scary for you, but we're going to get to the bottom of it. You'll be sleeping like babies again in no time!"

"No one was crying," said Myrtle. "And, I feel like I ought to clarify, the tub was definitely empty. Someone refilled it."

"Pipes can hold a lot of water," said the officer. "All that water you saw was probably from earlier, or was residual water that was still in the pipes. I'm fourth generation Windy Pines, and this is a safe community. I never should have said *foul play* just now. I can see how that alarmed you two. My bad."

"You're fourth generation?" asked Myrtle, a little more interested in him now. "What did you say your name was?"

"Wells. I'm Travis Wells."

"How *about* that?" said Myrtle, delighted. "So, that must make you Franny Baker's nephew?"

"I sure am! How'd you know that?" asked Travis.

"I know everyone in this town," said Myrtle. "My mother's mother was a Fillmore, and as you probably know..."

"The Fillmores founded this town," said Officer Wells.

Myrtle beamed. "That's right," she said.

"You know, I used to work at this inn back when I was in junior high and high school. I was one of the kids who mowed the lawn," said Officer Wells. "Mr. Peterman was a real hard ass. Either you liked him or you hated him. I think he's the reason I'm a cop now. He always told me 'Work harder, you little maggot! Do it right the first time, you little shit for brains.' That kind of encouragement doesn't work for everyone, but it worked for me. I guess since I never really had a father figure."

"Huh," said Klarinda, nodding awkwardly. She'd heard plenty of other stories like this about Ralph Peterman. He wasn't exactly Mr. Popularity around Windy Pines.

"I'm twenty-four and half now, so it's been quite a few years since then..." Travis Wells continued.

Twenty-four and a half, Klarinda repeated in her head, grimacing to herself. She'd never met anyone over the age of ten who counted their age in halves.

"Awe, that was right before I started working here," said Myrtle. "I came on about, oh, six or seven years ago now. I lived up in Billings for years. Then I realized one day that it was time to come back home to Windy Pines. But if I'd been here when you were here I would have remembered you! So then, you must be related to Gertie and Richard?"

Realizing she now had no one on her side, Klarinda stepped into the dining room to check on Benji and Christopher, who were playing a game of checkers and having some hot chocolate, trying to pass time.

"Can I get either of you anything?" asked Klarinda.

"Nothing for me," said Benji, scowling.

"I wouldn't mind some cookies, if you've got some," said Christopher.

"Let me see what I can come up with for you," said Klarinda. She stepped back out into the front hallway where Myrtle and Officer Wells were still chatting about local gossip. Her presence seemed to remind the young officer that he could be doing a little more to get to the bottom of things.

"Mind if I have a word with your remaining guests?" he asked Klarinda, whipping out his little notebook again, back to being all-business.

"Go right ahead," she said, "but please be nice to them. As you can imagine, they've been through quite the ordeal and are going on very little sleep. Like all of us."

"Oh, I'll be nice," he said. "But if either of them is hiding anything, I'll get to the bottom of it. Just you wait and see!"

Chapter 14

"I hope you like chocolate chip cookies," Klarinda told Christopher, setting a plate of them down on the table in front of him.

"Fresh baked? I wasn't expecting homemade cookies! I would have been happy with some Chips Ahoy!"

"Well, they aren't exactly from scratch. Pierre had some ready-to-go dough in the fridge so I just had to put them on a pan and throw them in the oven. I figured it's the least I can do for you and Benji, all things considered. Speaking of Benji, is she still talking with the officer?"

Christopher nodded, his mouth full of a bite of cookie. "Sorry," he said after he'd swallowed it. "I guess I'm hungrier than I thought."

"Not me," said Klarinda, picturing Lannie, whose body was still waiting in her bedroom for the coroner's arrival. "I may never eat again. So, how long have Benji and Officer Wells been talking?"

"Since right after you were in here asking if we needed anything. How long ago was that? Maybe twenty minutes ago. What did you say the last name of the officer was?" he added, stuffing another cookie in his mouth.

"Wells. Officer Travis Wells."

"That's me," said the officer, stepping from the parlor into the dining room. "I smelled these cookies and I cut my interview with Brittany short," he said.

"Her name's Benji," said Klarinda, smiling blandly.

"Ooo-hee! Did you make these yourself?" Officer Wells asked Klarinda, taking several from the plate and making a little tower in his palm.

"Not exactly," she said. "Any word from the coroner or the sheriff, or any of the other officers?"

"Haven't you heard? I guess I forget that everyone's not tuned into a police scanner twenty-four seven like I am! A snowplow crashed into the clock tower downtown and it went right through the front window of O'Malley's Diner! Terry Schwartz was sitting up front playing euchre and he wound up with a broken arm! He's lucky to be alive! As soon as I'm done here I'm going to head back down the hill into town and have a look. It sounds real exciting! Glad I got chains on my tires. These cookies, Miss Snow. Mmmm-eeeee."

Christopher Murdock stood up suddenly, clutching his stomach. He turned his head away from Klarinda and the officer, trying to hide the nauseous expression on his face. "Excuse me," he mumbled, darting through the dining room's doorway and heading for the restroom.

"What was that all about?" asked Officer Wells, popping another cookie in his mouth.

"I'm not sure," said Klarinda, "but he certainly didn't look good."

"Well, it's not the cookies. I can tell you that. These are the best darn cookies I've ever had."

"I hope he's alright," she said. "By the way, where's Benji?"

"She said she was going to go upstairs to her room and lie down," said the officer.

"Seriously? No one's supposed to be upstairs. When I talked to the restoration company that our insurance adjuster put me in touch with, they said that it's not safe to be up there. They said that kind of damage can compromise the whole building. If we weren't trapped in here it would probably be better to not even be inside this place right now."

The officer laughed. "This old place looks pretty solid to me." He stood up and dusted off his hands, sprinkling cookie crumbs all over the floor. "Well," he said. "I hope the rest of your day isn't as exciting as your morning and last night were."

"It looks like you're leaving?" asked Klarinda.

"I sure am. I've got to see O'Malley's in person!"

"Aren't you going to talk to Christopher?"

"He's sick, right?"

"Well, yes, but he'll come out of the restroom eventually."

"I don't think it's that important for me to talk to him," said the officer.

"If it was important to talk to Benji, isn't it also important to talk to Christopher?"

"If there wasn't something bigger going on downtown, I'd stick around. But duty calls," said Officer Wells. He went out to the front hall and took his coat and hat from the coat rack by the front door. "Be careful," he said as he zipped up his coat. "This place seems to be experiencing an unlucky spell."

"That might be the biggest understatement I've ever heard," said Klarinda.

Officer Wells opened the front door of the inn, letting in a treacherous gust of wind and snow. He pulled his hat down a little lower and winked as he stepped out onto the front porch. "Don't worry," he said, his words nearly blowing away. "At this point, I think the odds are pretty good that Mistletoe Manor has had all the bad luck one place can take. Things can only get better."

Chapter 15

The plate and crumbs had been cleared away. So had the mugs of cold cocoa and the abandoned game of checkers. It had been ten minutes since Officer Wells left, and there was still no sign of any other officers. Christopher Murdock had not emerged from the restroom and Benji had not come down from her room. Pierre and Myrtle were both resting in their own small apartments behind the inn, and Klarinda had no intention of disturbing them.

Not sure what to do with herself, and having to avoid her own apartment since it was a disaster zone housing a dead body, she decided to take Pumpernickel outside for a potty break.

She'd just clicked the little dog's leash to her collar when she remembered that the Yorkie-poo was accustomed to wearing a tiny quilted coat when she went outside. Klarinda hesitated, but then decided she'd better get the dog's coat. She went upstairs, let herself into Lannie's room, and quietly closed the door behind her. "While I'm in here, I might as well do a little detective work," she told herself.

She wasn't sure what she was looking for, but she figured she'd know it when she found it. First, she unzipped Lannie's suitcase and took a look inside. Aside from expensive brands of clothing, there wasn't much of interest. She sniffed around inside the bag, but all it smelled like were freshly laundered clothing and perfume. She found two of Pumpernickel's coats and a few designer leashes, and she set these aside. Bored with the luggage, she unzipped Lannie's purse. Inside it were a variety of anti-anxiety medications, stress relief creams, and a velvet bag labeled *Healing Stones and Crystals*. Inside the bag were colorful stones and some crystals, exactly as described. She opened Lannie's wallet. It held numerous credit cards, nearly one thousand dollars cash, and a variety of coffee shop punch cards. In the little plastic holder in the front of the wallet was a picture of Lannie and the very attractive man who most likely was her husband Tom. They were dressed up like they were at a wedding or some other fancy event, and they appeared to be head over heels in love. Klarinda turned on the lamp to study it a little more closely, just as the door squeaked open.

Klarinda and Benji both jumped and screamed at once.

"Oh my goodness! We can't jump up here," Klarinda exclaimed, clutching her hand to her chest and looking around in a wild-eyed panic. "I'm afraid the whole place is going to come tumbling down," she explained.

"That's crazy," Benji said.

Klarinda stuffed Lannie's wallet back into her purse and set the purse where she'd found it on the sofa. She picked up Pumpernickel's coats. "What are you doing in here?" she asked Benji, regaining her composure.

"What are *you* doing in here?" asked Benji.

"Looking around. After all, I own this place," Klarinda said, giving Benji a nudge out of the way as she stepped back out of Lannie's suite and into the hallway. She took the master key from her pocket and locked the door. "We shouldn't be up here. I'm going back downstairs and you should too."

"You might own this place," said Benji, "but you don't own me."

"Don't you think it's a little creepy? Sitting up here all alone, with everything that has gone on here in the past day?"

"Everything about this place is creepy," snapped Benji. "I feel safer up here in my room than down there with you and those other losers."

"Fine. Suit yourself," said Klarinda.

She went back downstairs and found Pumpernickel napping on the ottoman in front of the fireplace in the parlor. Christopher was still nowhere to be seen. Klarinda tried to block out the bad feeling in the pit of her stomach telling her to check on him. Instead, she dressed the little dog in her coat and they went outside.

It was nearing dinner time and the lights of Windy Pines were glowing in the windows of the little shops and homes down the hill. Normally Klarinda enjoyed being up here and having a view of the small town, but tonight she shivered, wishing she could relocate the inn and nestle it down there in the midst of the village instead of being perched partway up this mountain, alone.

"Are you all set?" she asked the tiny pup, scooping her up and turning to go back inside, when something caught her attention. She tucked Pumpernickel inside her coat and began stumbling through the snow to where Christopher's car was parked, wanting to be sure her eyes weren't playing tricks on her. As she thought she'd seen, there were tracks plunged through the deep snow, connecting Christopher's car to the side of the inn. Someone had trekked from the door off the kitchen, around the side of the inn, to his car.

His driver's side window was partially cleared off as well. She reached out her hand to open the car door and discovered that it was unlocked. The car was empty inside, except that the duffle bag Christopher had arrived with was now resting on the passenger seat.

Klarinda looked around at the gusting, frigid parking lot, confused. If Christopher had wanted to put his duffle bag in his car, why wouldn't he have gone out the front door? And why would he want to put anything in the car, when he'd probably be stuck at the inn for at least another night? She examined the tracks again. They looked quite big, and quite new, but were already refilling with snow. Klarinda peered a little closer at the footprints, realizing that the person who made the path had taken that exact same return path back to the kitchen.

"Well, obviously," she told herself, "or they'd still be out here." But why go to all that trouble when you could walk out the front door and get to the vehicle by going through just a couple of inches of snow, instead of nearly two feet of it?

She was considering unzipping the duffle bag and taking a look inside, when Pumpernickel shivered and let out a tiny whimper. "Let's get out of here," she agreed, closing the car door and trudging back to the inn.

On her way back, she did her best to kick snow into the shallow tracks she'd made in the plowed part of the parking lot. When she got to the front door of the inn, she looked back at her footprints. With the snow continuing to fall and blow, the evidence of her having investigated Christopher's car was rapidly disappearing.

Chapter 16

"I'm so glad I have a load of clothes down here," Klarinda told Myrtle, as she pulled a pile of jeans, sweatshirts, and pajamas from the dryer, "because I don't ever want to go back into my apartment."

"Way to find a silver lining," laughed Myrtle, balancing on a stepladder, reaching for an old electric fan that was up on one of the shelves in the basement.

"I never thought I'd say this, but it's a good thing we don't have air conditioning here at the inn."

"That's right," said Myrtle. "These fans are coming in handy."

"Please be careful," said Klarinda. "I really can't handle much more today."

"I'm being careful," Myrtle assured her, stretching. Her hand had just closed on the fan when a spider raced across her knuckles. She screamed and grabbed the shelf, yanking it forward with a jolt, and jumping back just in time to avoid being crushed beneath it.

Klarinda dropped her laundry into the basket in front of the dryer and ran to Myrtle's side.

"I'm fine! I'm fine. I'm okay. I'm fine," Myrtle gasped, trying to reassure both Klarinda and herself that she really was alright.

"You just about gave me a heart attack," said Klarinda.

Myrtle laughed weakly. "Me too. I just about gave myself a heart attack." She dusted herself off and shook her head. "Look at this mess I've made," she said.

"Oh, please, Myrtle. This pile of garbage is the least of our worries."

"I'll clean it up," Myrtle said. "We're going to need some help getting this shelf set back up, though."

"We don't need half this junk, and we certainly don't need to worry about cleaning it up tonight. This is all stuff left here from the Petermans'. Most of it's mildew-covered and moldy and should have been thrown away a long time ago. Like this, for instance," said Klarinda, holding up a rickety chalet style birdhouse. "Or this," she said, about an open cardboard box of plastic forks, filled with mouse droppings. "Or whatever's in here," she said, opening a plain cardboard box that had been up on the top of the metal shelf, but that now lay on its side on the basement floor. Inside was something made of paper. Stacks and stacks of... envelopes.

Klarinda froze, a shiver of recognition running down her spine. Plain white envelopes. She opened the flaps of the box wider and discovered matching cards with an elegant embossment. She pulled one of the cards from the box. "Funny," she said to Myrtle, "but these cards seem to be popping up everywhere lately."

"Haven't you ever seen those before?" asked Myrtle.

"Not before yesterday when all our guests showed up with them."

Myrtle cocked her head to the side, confused. "They used to use those all the time here. As thank you notes, as invitations, just for general correspondence. I forgot about those cards, but Ellen Peterman was real big on them. Are you telling me that the guests from that academy all showed up with these same cards?"

"That's what I'm telling you," said Klarinda.

"I don't get it," said Myrtle. "Could they have all been invited here by the Petermans? Many years ago?"

"And they're all just arriving now?" asked Klarinda.

Myrtle shrugged. "I don't know," she said.

"We'll figure it out," Klarinda said, going back to her pile of laundry and changing from her wet, snow-cuffed jeans into a warm, dry pair. "But for now, let's not mention that we found these. Let's close the box back up, put them in the corner, and pretend we never found them."

"Okay," said Myrtle, doing as she was told, "but why so secretive?"

"I'm not sure why," Klarinda admitted, "but I just don't think we should talk about it."

"Fair enough," said Myrtle.

"And the shelf," said Klarinda. "We'll deal with it later. For now, I'd rather have you upstairs by me. I think we should stick together. Pierre, too."

"You're giving me the willies," Myrtle said, laughing nervously and shivering a little.

"Sorry," said Klarinda. "Call me paranoid. But would you mind getting Pierre and having him hang out with us? We could all play a game to make the time go by a little faster. At some point the police will have to show up again. Until then, I'd rather us be in one place where we can keep an eye on each other."

"I'll get him," Myrtle agreed.

"I'll be in the parlor with our guests," said Klarinda. "Well, hopefully, anyway," she added, silently praying that Christopher's bout of food poisoning hadn't turned out to be deadly.

Chapter 17

"You're still alive," Benji said to Christopher. Was Klarinda imagining things, or did Benji look a little surprised?

"I'm still alive," he agreed, then moaned and turned over and pulled a quilt over his head. He had taken over the sofa in the parlor.

"Since our dining room's closed and we're all looking for something to do…" Klarinda said.

"We are?" asked Pierre.

"I thought we could play a game or two of Skip-Bo," Klarinda continued. "It's the perfect game for five players."

"Are the police ever coming back, or what's happening here?" asked Christopher.

"I just heard from Deputy Franklin, and he said that the coroner and hopefully some officers should be here by nine o'clock."

"Yay! The coroner's coming," said Benji, in a sarcastic singsong.

"Is that Officer Wells coming back?" asked Christopher, queasily sitting up.

"I'm not sure which officers are coming," said Klarinda. "Why do you ask?"

"Just asking," he said. "Actually, I was thinking of putting some chains on my tires and heading out of here. No offense, Klarinda, but I've had about as much as I can take of this vacation. My Subaru's got four wheel drive. It's tougher than it looks. But if I'm going to put the chains on, I might need some help."

"Why does it have to be Officer Wells?" asked Benji.

"It doesn't," said Christopher.

"I don't know which officers will be here," said Klarinda. "We could request for him to come out here if you'd like."

"No, don't do that," Christopher said quickly. "I don't want to be a pain in the ass."

"How are you planning to leave? Aren't all the roads closed?" asked Benji.

"They might be closed to the general public," said Christopher, "but you can bet some vehicles are still using them."

Pierre set his bottle of beer down on one of the crocheted doilies that Klarinda had provided for the guests to use as coasters. "Are we going to play this game, or can I go back to my apartment and watch the rest of *Survivor*?"

"Why watch it when you can live it?" asked Benji.

"Give me those cards," Myrtle instructed, holding out her hand. She shuffled them and dealt out twenty cards to herself and the four people sitting around her.

"I don't know how to play this," said Pierre, shaking his head at the cards and looking anything but pleased to be there.

"You'll catch right on," Klarinda promised.

"At least you got a Christmas tree, but it still doesn't feel very festive around here," said Benji.

"Gee. You think?" said Christopher.

"We ought to play some Christmas music," said Benji. "I pictured this place having Christmas music playing all the time."

"We used to have a radio in here, but it broke," said Klarinda. "Why don't you sing that song you were singing last night," she suggested to Christopher. "The one about the snow angels and candy canes?"

"What song?" asked Benji.

"I'd had a little to drink last night," said Christopher. "I'm not in the mood to sing right now."

"Go ahead, sing it," Myrtle said to Christopher.

"I'm not feeling up to it," said Christopher.

"Then I'll sing it," said Myrtle. "Now, how did it go?"

"I don't remember," said Christopher. "I was just making it up. It was just some dumb song."

"It was good," Myrtle insisted. She cleared her throat, and gave it a try: "Mistletoe Manor, up on the hill... Spreading good cheer and spreading good will... Snow angels on the lawn and candy canes on the tree... Mistletoe Manor, book a room for me!"

Klarinda applauded.

"You didn't make that up," Pierre said to Christopher.

"I think I did," he said. "Are we going to play this game or what?"

"That's the old Mistletoe Manor commercial. From about ten or twelve years ago."

"Oh. Is it?" asked Christopher.

Pierre nodded. "It sure is."

"I guess I heard it before and it got stuck in my head," said Christopher.

Just then Klarinda and the others heard the front door of the inn open, immediately followed by the sound of men's voices.

"Hello? Anybody here?" asked a gruff voice.

"We're in here," said Klarinda, going to meet them. She closed the pocket doors after herself, figuring Myrtle, Pierre, and her guests could use a break from the ongoing drama.

Deputy Franklin and the sheriff stood in the front hallway of the inn. "I'm Sheriff Carter," said the older man, holding out his hand to Klarinda. "I don't believe we've met."

"I'm so glad you're here," said Klarinda, shaking his hand. "I'm Klarinda Snow, innkeeper. Hello again, Deputy Franklin."

"Hello," he said, just as the door opened again and the coroner stepped inside.

"Hello again, Klarinda," said the coroner.

"It's a relief to see you," she said. "I'll show you to... umm... the accident." She led the men down the hallway and to the right, and then gestured toward her apartment. There was no way she was going back in there. All three men disappeared inside, and she returned to the parlor to check on her guests.

"Everyone okay in here?" she asked.

"We're fine," said Myrtle.

"Where's Christopher?" asked Klarinda.

"His stomach was acting up again," said Pierre.

"I think we ought to ask those policemen to take us down the mountain so we can check in at a real hotel," said Benji. "I don't see any point in staying here another night."

"I'm perfectly content to stay in my own apartment," said Pierre.

"Me too," said Myrtle.

Klarinda sighed. She had no idea what her plan was. She certainly didn't intend to sleep in her apartment. Ever again, perhaps. And now that Christopher had taken over the sofa in here... She wasn't sure what she was going to do. Benji's plan didn't sound half bad. She shoved the quilt to the side and sat down on the sofa, and immediately shot back up.

"What's the matter?" asked Myrtle.

"It's wet," she said, pressing her palm against the cushion, to make sure she wasn't imagining things.

"Did he spill his hot chocolate on it?" asked Benji.

"No. It's wet, but it doesn't look like it's stained. It's just wet with… water," said Klarinda, sliding over to a dry spot.

"Would you mind coming in here?" asked Deputy Franklin, appearing in the doorway between the front hall and the parlor.

"Me?" asked Klarinda, jumping up.

"Yes," he said, turning and walking away.

She scrambled along after him, all the way back to her apartment. The sheriff and the coroner were in the doorway to her bedroom.

"You want me to go back in there?" she asked, over the sound of whirring fans.

"Why are the windows open?" asked the sheriff.

"Myrtle must have opened them a crack. The guy from the restoration company told us we needed to dry everything out as quickly as possible, to reduce long-term damage to the inn."

The sheriff nodded. "With all these open windows, you'll be lucky if the pipes back here don't freeze and give you even more problems."

"I didn't realize…" Klarinda said, but was interrupted by the sheriff again.

"Can you explain this?" he asked, pointing to a clean strip of wood floor in the midst of a puddle of dried blood.

"I'm not sure what that is. I'd really rather not come back in here," she said, trying not to look at Lannie's body.

"It looks like there was a rope, or a belt, or something of that nature attached to the foot of the bed, but that whatever it was has been removed, leaving an outline," said the sheriff, pointing to the foot of the bed, directly beneath where the bathtub had plunged through the ceiling.

"I didn't see anything like that," said Klarinda. "Then again, I didn't stick around in here. As soon as I saw what had happened, I ran out of here and haven't come back since." She looked up through the open ceiling, at the medicine cabinet and cheery striped curtains in the yellow guestroom's bathroom. It was rather surreal to be able to simply *see* it all like this. She rubbed her hands up and down her arms, fighting back against the chill in the room and the nightmarish reality of it all.

"Are you cold?" asked Deputy Franklin.

"Yes, of course," she said.

"Who did you say opened these windows and put the fans in here?" the sheriff asked.

"Myrtle put them in here earlier today. We were trying to dry out the ceiling."

"Why would there have been something *tied* to your bed?" asked Deputy Franklin.

"Are you into the kinkier lifestyle?" asked the sheriff. "Not that I'm judging you. I'm just asking."

"No," said Klarinda, her cheeks growing hot. "I have no idea why anything would have been tied to the bed."

"What was this guest doing in your room, way back here in the corner of your apartment, anyway?" asked the sheriff.

"She was looking for her dog. She came in here at the exact moment the floor collapsed."

"What was her dog doing in here?"

"I don't know. It just ended up in here, I guess," said Klarinda.

"Don't you normally keep your apartment locked?" asked the deputy.

"Well, sometimes. Not always. I'm often running in and out of here throughout the day, and with just seven guestrooms here at the inn, I don't usually worry too much about security."

"Interesting," said the sheriff. "Do you mind if we look around a little?"

"I don't mind," said Klarinda, "but am I in trouble? I feel like you're acting as though you're suspicious of me."

"Should we be?" asked Deputy Franklin.

"No! Of course not," said Klarinda.

The sheriff was already nosing around on Klarinda's dresser, opening her jewelry box and the small lidded basket that held her hair clips. Next he began opening the drawers of her dresser.

"Is this really necessary?" she asked, watching in dismay as he picked up a handful of her underwear and looked underneath them. "I can assure you, Sheriff Carter, there's nothing of any importance in there."

"Seeing as how five people have died at this inn in the past twenty-four hours, I'd say that we have reason to be concerned," said the sheriff.

"I concur," said the coroner.

"If you're so concerned, why have you all left us here alone with a dead body all day? We could have used your help a lot earlier than this. It's been a long, frightening day for my guests and me."

"Guests?" asked the sheriff, pausing from his treasure hunt. "Isn't there only one guest left? I saw Officer Wells's notes. The only guest he mentioned was some nerdy little lady named Brittany. Apparently she was rude as hell, but he determined she wasn't capable of hurting a fly. He said all she wanted to do was talk about how she was going to give this place a bad review on something or another called Yelp. And then he said she bragged about how smart she was and told him that cops have notoriously low IQs. She said it right to his face!"

"That sounds like her," said Klarinda. "But there are two guests left. Benjamina McKellar is her name – not Brittany like you guys keep calling her -- and Christopher Murdock."

"And this Christopher Murdock… He's *alive*? Or is that the name of another one of the casualties?" asked Deputy Franklin.

"He's alive," said Klarinda.

"We've got to get Travis to take better notes," said the sheriff.

"Would you like to speak to Christopher or Benji?" Klarinda asked the officers, desperate to get their ill-directed focus off herself and her underwear drawer.

"That sounds like a good idea," said the sheriff. "Deputy Franklin, here, will sit down with them while the coroner and I remove this deceased guest from the premises."

"You're going to remove her?"

"Yes," said the sheriff. And then, in what Klarinda considered to be a rather snotty tone, "Is that okay with you?"

"It's more than okay," she said.

"First though, I think it's best if we take some photos of the room. Just in case we need them later," said the sheriff.

"Go right ahead," said Klarinda.

"Why don't you show me to this Christopher person," said Deputy Franklin, "since it seems he's avoided nearly every interview we've conducted here."

"Sure. Follow me," she said, leading the deputy back to the parlor. She opened the pocket doors that led from the front hallway to the parlor, revealing Benji, Myrtle, and Pierre immersed in a game of Skip-bo. A fire was dancing in the fireplace and *Silver Bells* was playing on the radio that Pierre had brought in from the kitchen. Pumpernickel looked up from her spot on the ottoman, sighed an adorable, tiny sigh, and went back to sleep.

"How quaint," said Deputy Franklin. "Are you Christopher?"

"No," said Pierre. "I'm the chef here at Mistletoe Manor. I have been for over a dozen years."

"Is that right? So you must see everything that goes on around here?" asked Deputy Franklin, not bothering to hide the aggression in his voice.

You're looking less hot all the time, Klarinda thought, deciding she'd go back to focusing her attention on Todd Healy.

"Not really," said Pierre. "I'm in the kitchen most of the time, or my apartment, right behind the inn. I'm a homebody. I don't go out much. I don't even have a car. I've already been interviewed by a different officer. Am I in some kind of trouble?"

"No," said the deputy. "No one's in any trouble. What about you?" he said, turning to face Benji. "Are you the one that told Officer Wells that police officers have low IQs?"

"I'm the one *who* told Officer Wells that police officers have low IQs," said Benji. "And I was only stating a fact. If you were smarter, you'd know I'm right. Am I under arrest for saying that, or is it still a free country?"

"Why don't you come into the dining room with me and we'll talk for a little bit," he suggested.

"No thanks," said Benji.

"Are you kidding me?" asked the deputy.

"I'm dead serious," she said.

Myrtle, Pierre, and Klarinda all exchanged looks of surprise.

"A lot of strange happenings have been going on here at Mistletoe Manor," Deputy Franklin said, his handsome, chiseled face growing red, "and we need to get to the bottom of it."

"Sometimes people are unfortunate," said Benji, "and accidents happen."

"I don't see why you won't sit down and talk to me," said the deputy, softening his tone a little.

"In the wrong hands, information can be twisted. Feeble minds can get confused," said Benji. "I'd rather not speak to you without the presence of a lawyer."

"A lawyer!" Deputy Franklin laughed. "No one needs to involve lawyers. I just want to talk to you."

"Is Christopher still in the bathroom?" asked Klarinda. "I'm asking because I think someone ought to interview *him* for a change."

"He went running off again," said Myrtle.

"Excuse me," the sheriff interrupted, standing in the doorway between the parlor and the hall. "We've got a lot of plaster crumbling down into the bedroom of your apartment. Is someone walking around upstairs? If so, get them out of there. A hole that big can do a lot to destroy the stability of a building this old."

"I'll see if Christopher's up there," said Klarinda, getting up and going to the hallway. She tentatively tiptoed up the stairs, expecting each step to bring down the entire inn.

"Oh, hi," said Christopher, just placing his hand on the top of the banister as Klarinda rounded the bend of the stairs.

"What are you doing up here?" asked Klarinda.

"Nothing. Just using the bathroom," he said.

"No one should be up here. In fact," she said, "I think it would be best if you cleared out any of your remaining things that are still up here. I'll get Benji's bags, and that way neither of you will have to come up here again."

"Fine by me," said Christopher, heading down the stairs.

Klarinda went to Benji's room. The door was wide open and her backpack – the only piece of luggage she'd brought -- was packed. Klarinda checked the adjoining bathroom and saw that everything was removed from the vanity top and in perfect order. She stepped back into the orange room and picked up the bag off the floor, but then something told her to look inside. She carefully unzipped the side pocket of the backpack, and was surprised to discover that inside was one of the plain invitations like the other guests had shown her. She took a quick look at it, saw it was an exact match to what the others had received, and then put it back where she'd found it and rezipped the pocket.

Listening to make sure no one was approaching, she quickly unzipped the main compartment of the backpack. Inside it was a towel from the orange room's guest bathroom, wadded up. There was no mistaking the flowered, one of a kind hand towel.

"What the heck? Why is she stealing one of my towels?" Klarinda wondered to herself. She pulled the towel from the bag and in doing so, it opened up and a blood-crusted dog leash fell out onto the floor.

Chapter 18

"Where did everyone go?" Klarinda asked Myrtle, doing her best to keep her calm exterior intact.

"The coroner and the sheriff just left with Lannie's body."

"Fascinating," said Klarinda. "So they really removed her body?"

"They removed the rest of the bodies," said Myrtle. "Why would they stop now?"

"One minute it seems like they're going to arrest me for murder, and the next minute they decide it's not even a crime scene?"

Myrtle shrugged. "Aren't you kind of glad to have her out of there?" she lowered her voice, adding, "She was giving me the willies!"

"Me too," Klarinda admitted.

"Pierre went back to his apartment to take some aspirin," Myrtle continued. "He'll be back soon. Deputy Franklin finally got Benji to talk to him. I guess she couldn't resist his good looks. They're in the dining room right now."

"And where's Christopher Murdock?" asked Klarinda.

"Darned if I know," said Myrtle.

"What's that sound?" asked Klarinda.

"Sounds like someone's shoveling," said Myrtle. "Maybe Christopher got bored and decided to be a little help around here."

"I highly doubt that," said Klarinda, throwing on her boots and coat and heading outside. Christopher was out in the parking lot, using the inn's snow shovel to dig out his car.

"Rumor has it," he said brightly, when he saw Klarinda approaching, "the road north of here has opened back up!"

"I don't think that leaving right now is a good idea," she said.

"I don't think staying here is a good idea either," he said, reasonably.

"Well, suit yourself. But it's still very dangerous out here. Even if they've reopened the road."

Christopher stuck the snow shovel into the pile of snow to his side, and leaned on it for a moment to catch his breath. "Some people might say it's dangerous in there," he said, before picking the shovel back up and continuing to dig. His car was warming up and chunks of snow and ice were sliding down the windows, melting away. The snow and wind had finally stopped. For the first time in many days, Windy Pines was spookily still and quiet.

The front door of the inn opened then and Deputy Franklin stepped outside.

"I guess you heard," he called to Klarinda, as he made his way toward his truck, "the sheriff and the coroner took your guest Alanna away."

"I heard," she said, turning and starting across the parking lot. "Could you hold up for a minute, Deputy?"

"I can't," he said. "I just got a call about an accident out on Steep Chapel Road. It sounds like it might be serious."

"This is important," she said.

"What is it?" he asked, unable to hide his impatience.

Klarinda was by the deputy's side now, and she realized that the sound of shoveling had stopped. She looked back to see Christopher scooping ice and snow from his headlights.

"I found a leash. A blood-covered leash," she said to the deputy. She clutched his arm, forcing him to listen to her.

"You found a leash?" he repeated, far too loudly.

"Shhh!" she hissed. "Yes."

"Where did you find this blood-covered leash?" he asked, a little more quietly, but with an incredulous tone Klarinda couldn't miss.

"In Benji's bag."

"Interesting," said the deputy. "Can you show it to me?"

"It's upstairs, but I think before I do that, you'd better make an arrest first, before it's too late."

"Benji's not going anywhere," said the Deputy. "I just saw her inside, digging into a big bowl of ice cream, mumbling about typos on a menu." He nodded, picturing her. "As guilty as could be," he added.

"I'm not talking about arresting Benji," said Klarinda. "I'm talking about arresting Christopher Murdock."

Behind them was the sound of Christopher's car door closing. He shifted the car into gear and slowly began driving down the path he'd shoveled for himself. He waved amicably as he inched past them.

"You need to catch him," Klarinda said. "You need to go after him now," she told them Deputy.

"Now, you say you found a leash?"

"He's getting away!"

"What makes you think he's guilty if you found the leash in Benji's bag?" asked Deputy Franklin.

"Please! You need to go after him! Call your squad! He's heading north. At least that's what he said. Who knows where he's really going, though?"

"If he's heading out of town, he's going to have to head north. There's currently no other option," the deputy agreed, scratching his head and glancing at his watch.

"Please, Deputy Franklin," Klarinda begged. "Can't you please go after him? Or do I need to do it myself? I've got new snow tires on my truck."

She waited for him to call her bluff, but he just looked at her, unimpressed.

"Fine. I guess I'll take matters into my own hands." She stomped off in the direction of the garage, pulling the shovel Christopher had just used from the snowbank on her way past it. She began shoveling at the three foot high snowdrift in front of the garage door.

"This is ridiculous," said the deputy. "Let's go back inside and you show me this leash."

"Whatever you say," said Klarinda, throwing down her shovel. "A murderer is driving away right now and you don't even care."

Deputy Franklin begrudgingly picked up his police radio. "What kind of car was he driving?" he asked Klarinda. "I wasn't paying attention."

"A green Subaru Outback with Montana license plates," she said. "I'm not sure what year it is. Not brand new. Maybe five or ten years old?"

"I'll call it in, but you'd better be right," he said.

Chapter 19

"Get these handcuffs off me! Get them off me right now!" Benji hollered, thrashing against the stair railing.

"Is this really necessary?" asked Klarinda. "She's not guilty. I have about twenty reasons why it could only be Christopher, if you'd just hear me out."

"Would you quit trying to outthink me?" Deputy Franklin said to Klarinda. "And you! Relax," he told Benji.

"I've got to agree with the deputy that if you wouldn't mind preserving my lovely wooden railing, I'd really appreciate it," Klarinda whispered.

"You can both go to hell!" screamed Benji. "Call me a lawyer."

"You're a lawyer. Ha ha," said Deputy Franklin.

"Real professional," said Klarinda. "Have you heard back from any of the other officers? Have they caught the actual murderer yet?"

Deputy Franklin gave Klarinda a warning look, refusing to answer her.

"I think we need to hear Klarinda out," Myrtle said.

"I'm with Klarinda," said Pierre. "With everything that's gone on here, Christopher shouldn't have been allowed to leave. Why'd you let him drive off like that?"

"Fine," said Deputy Franklin. He turned to Klarinda. "Spit it out. Why do you think that Christopher is guilty, when the only piece of evidence we have is a bloody leash, found in *this* woman's bag?"

"Why would she have hidden it in her own bag?" Klarinda said.

"Thank you," said Benji.

"Because maybe she's not that bright," said the deputy.

"I have a one sixty IQ. I went to Harvard on a full scholarship. I'm an international spelling bee champion. What else do you need to know about me?" yelled Benji.

"Why were you invited here, when you never attended the same boarding school as the rest of them?" asked the deputy.

"You got me," said Benji.

"Do you want to hear my evidence about Christopher or not?" asked Klarinda.

"Go right ahead," said the deputy.

"Okay," said Klarinda. All eyes were on her. "First of all," she said, trying to keep her voice from shaking, "he had a connection to Mistletoe Manor. He proved that when he knew the old commercial that hadn't played for years."

"So he knew some commercial," said the deputy. "So what?"

"Well, whoever brought this group together wouldn't have picked this inn out of the blue. They had to have some connection. I think Christopher was a lawn boy here. I think he worked with Officer Wells, and that's why every time Travis Wells came around, Christopher would rush off pretending to have stomach cramps."

"That's quite the stretch," said Deputy Franklin.

"Maybe," said Klarinda, "but it explains why he was so surprised to see me when he first showed up here. He was asking me whether this was my place. I think he was expecting to find his old boss, Mr. Peterman. I think Christopher had a whole list of people he was getting revenge on. Plenty of people hated Mr. Peterman. He was notoriously cruel to his staff. I think if Ralph Peterman was still the innkeeper of Mistletoe Manor, he'd also be dead right now."

Myrtle and Pierre looked at each other and each gave small nods of agreement. "He wasn't the nicest guy to work for, and he was even worse to the kids who worked here in the summer," Pierre agreed.

"Whoever arranged this had access to the basement here, at some point, when those old invitations got stolen," Klarinda added.

"There used to be stacks of them in the guestrooms and the parlor for guests to use if they wanted to write letters while they were staying here," said Myrtle. "Sorry to contradict you," she added, "but any guest could have gotten a hold of a pile of them."

"But the ones that arrived here all smelled musty," said Klarinda. "I'm pretty sure they came from that box of extras in the basement."

"Why would Christopher want to murder his old friends?" asked the deputy.

"Maybe because they were all a bunch of assholes," said Benji.

"Or," said Klarinda, "maybe because they were all more successful than him. Or maybe he had been in love with Avery Burtz?"

"With who?" asked the deputy.

"Never mind," said Klarinda. "The point is, he hated bullies. In fact, he even had a shirt that said so! And he was here to eradicate them."

"And where does she fit in to all of this?" asked the deputy, nodding toward Benji.

"Did you ever bully Christopher Murdock?" Myrtle asked Benji.

"How dare you accuse me of anything?" spat Benji, making poor Myrtle jump back in surprise. "I've never bullied anyone," the orange haired young woman declared.

"You've bullied me!" said Deputy Franklin.

"Me too," said Myrtle. "You tore me apart just a half hour ago when I forgot to bring you a spoon with your ice cream. And honestly, I'm feeling a little bullied right now."

"And you sent your ice cream back to the kitchen because I forgot to put rainbow sprinkles on it," said Pierre.

"That's not bullying. It's quality control," said Benji.

"Call it what you will," said Klarinda, "and I'd also call it bullying, but I still think you're innocent."

"So," the deputy said to Benji, "tell us where you fit in to all this."

"Maybe Christopher Murdock had issues with me. Personal issues. I've seen it before," said Benji. "Many, many times, in fact. Maybe I beat him out of some scholarship we both applied for. Maybe he came in second to me in some spelling bee when we were kids. I think that's it. He brought me here to get even with me. He brought me here to frame me! I'm the real victim in all this!"

"Do you have any other evidence against Christopher for me?" Deputy Franklin asked Klarinda.

"Besides him hurrying out of here, and trying to hide that he intended to leave... I don't know. Let me think," she said.

"Do you realize," said the deputy, "that you haven't actually explained how any of the murders were committed?"

Klarinda turned to Deputy Franklin. "Most of them weren't very complex. I can't imagine that tipping over an armoire on someone or drowning two drunken people is that difficult. Also, there's something Benji said that resonated with me."

"What's that?" asked Benji, perking up a little from hearing her name mentioned.

"Well," said Klarinda, "you were talking about statistics. Which got me to thinking."

"Go on," said the deputy.

"The odds of having this many accidents in one place within twenty-four hours or so has got to be about one in a million."

"Or one in a billion," said Benji.

"And," Klarinda continued, "if we're looking at statistics, most violent crimes are committed by men. Most murders are committed by men. And most serial killers are men. We're talking the *vast* majority. It's not even close."

"Oh, really?" asked Deputy Franklin.

"Well, yes. Really," said Klarinda. "I took a criminal justice class once in college, and I got an A plus."

Benji and the deputy both snickered at Klarinda's proclamation, and then simultaneously clamped their mouths shut and glared at one another.

"I hate to make sweeping generalizations, but what I'm saying happens to be true," Klarinda added.

"None of this helps with the leash, which is our only real piece of evidence."

"Maybe Christopher tied Pumpernickel in there, knowing it would be a way to lure Lannie in there. The floor was probably so soggy by that point that all he had to do was to give it a couple of kicks before it caved in. Especially with that full tub of water resting on it. Lannie would have been kneeling down there to unfasten Pumpernickel and would have been situated exactly under the tub. And that's when the floor gave way."

"How did he get the timing right? There was only a few seconds when Lannie would have been right there, setting her dog free," said the deputy.

"Maybe he was listening for her? Or maybe he was really lucky. Or maybe his target was actually Pumpernickel?" Klarinda suggested.

"Maybe," scoffed Deputy Franklin. "Maybe, maybe, maybe," he added.

"Are *you* going to do any of the detective work, or is it all up to me?" Klarinda snapped.

"This isn't detective work! It's a guessing game. I'm ashamed to even be a part of this debacle," said the deputy.

"How can you say that?" asked Klarinda. "I've basically solved your crime for you. You just need to fill in the missing pieces."

"You acted like you had this case buttoned up," said Deputy Franklin. "You've got our officers risking their lives to track down someone who you claim is guilty of five murders. Do you realize how serious of an accusation that is? I'm still not convinced that there have even been any crimes committed here."

"Back to Christopher Murdock," said Klarinda. "Have they caught him yet?"

"Let me check," he said. "I'll be right back." And then he stepped out the front door of the inn. "Give me a minute," he said, closing the front door after him.

Chapter 20

"Klarinda, are you sure you're right about all of this?" asked Myrtle.

She, Pierre, and Klarinda had closed themselves off in the parlor, leaving Benji handcuffed to the stairs.

"Christopher has unquestionably been sneaking around. He took his duffle bag down to his car, using the side door off the kitchen, instead of going out the front door. He *knew* he was checking out early, and he went out of his way to hide it," said Klarinda.

"You're sure about that?" asked Myrtle.

"Yes," said Klarinda. "I saw the tracks in the snow and his duffle bag sitting on the passenger seat of his car. Then he came back in, pretending it hadn't happened, but the couch was all wet where he'd been lying, which makes sense, since there must have been snow caked all over his jeans."

"But why go through the whole inn and out the kitchen door when he could more easily sneak right out the front door?" asked Myrtle.

"Good question!" said Klarinda.

"The odds of him being seen by one of us were greater if he went through the kitchen than out the front door," Pierre agreed.

"I'll admit that it doesn't make a whole lot of sense," said Klarinda.

"Unless there was something in the kitchen he wanted," Myrtle suggested.

Pierre caught his breath, and nodded.

"What is it?" asked Klarinda.

"That could explain what happened to the two bags of potato chips that were in the kitchen. They're both gone."

"If he stole the chips, that would make more sense why he was in the kitchen and sneaking out that door," said Myrtle.

"So he *is* guilty... of stealing... chips," said Klarinda. Suddenly, she thought of the pile of cash. Ten thousand dollars in neatly stacked bills. Would someone who could so easily part with ten thousand dollars be driving an old car, asking how to redeem plane tickets, and stealing chips? It seemed unlikely. Although maybe if he were a real cheapskate... She swallowed. "I'm getting confused," she admitted.

"Either way," said Myrtle, "it's a good thing they went after him. There are plenty of unanswered questions."

"It was shady of him to rush out like that," said Pierre.

"Or maybe he's innocent, and he felt like his life depended on getting out of here. I mean, it would be a reasonable assumption for someone to make," said Klarinda.

"Your theory about him could still be right," said Myrtle.

"I don't know anymore," Klarinda admitted. She buried her face in her hands, before coming back up for air a moment later. "It all made so much sense to me, but now I'm having doubts. I'm exhausted. It doesn't help that these police don't seem to know what they're doing or care very much about the outcome."

Just then the pocket doors flew open. "You'll be happy to hear that Christopher Murdock's escape journey has been halted," Deputy Franklin announced.

"Are you serious?" asked Klarinda.

"I'm very, very serious," said the deputy. "You don't know me very well, but if you did, you'd know I never joke around. Ever."

"Fun," muttered Klarinda.

The front door of the inn flew open again and Officer Travis Wells came running in. "I got here as soon as I could," he said. "I wasn't sure if I should go here or there, or what! So I came here since I was just down the road. What a wild night!" He turned to Klarinda, his face flushed with excitement, "I just heard on the scanner, Sheriff Carter is real pleased with you, Miss Snow!"

"So you caught Christopher? I guess now you can get to the bottom of things," Myrtle said to the officers.

"Do you want us to all come down to the police station?" Pierre suggested. "Our evening is ruined anyway, and I wouldn't mind a change of scenery."

"There won't be any need for that," said the deputy. "Christopher Murdock's car got crushed beneath an avalanche, just north of town. It's anyone's guess whether they'll be able to dig him out of his car in time to save him."

"As I see it," said Travis Wells, nodding enthusiastically, "it's a win-win. A wanted, dead or alive, kind of situation."

Deputy Franklin nodded succinctly, turning his handsome face on Klarinda. "Good job," he said, rather sullenly.

"Um, yeah. I'm not so sure about that," she admitted.

"Don't get all humble on me," said the deputy. "Just take the compliment and let it go. Well, I think our work here is done for tonight."

"One question for you, Officer Wells, before you go," said Klarinda. "You saw Christopher Murdock when you were here earlier, even if you didn't interview him, right?"

"Uhh... I'm not sure if I actually saw him or not."

"You had to have seen him. When you came in for the cookies?"

"Oh, yeah. The sick guy. So *that's* who's trapped in the avalanche?"

"Yes. Same guy. When you saw him, did he seem familiar to you? Did you ever work with him here, maybe back when you were a lawn boy?"

"I never seen him before in my life," said Travis Wells.

"You're sure about that?" asked Klarinda. "Did you get a good look at him?"

"That guy who was always holding his stomach and running to the restroom? Yeah, I saw him. But he wasn't anyone I knew."

Klarinda nodded, silently.

"Any more questions?" asked Officer Wells.

"No," said Klarinda.

"Then we're outtie," Travis Wells declared, putting his hat back on.

"Could you please remember to unhandcuff Benji before you leave?" Myrtle said to the policemen.

"She wasn't there when I just came in. Not that I saw, anyway," said Deputy Franklin. He opened the parlor doors a little wider, peeked out, and shook his head. "Nope. Not there."

"Okie dokie. See you later," said Officer Wells.

"Where the heck is she?" exclaimed Myrtle. "You police officers had better stick around and help us find her!"

"I'm ready for some dinner," muttered Travis Wells.

"Of *course* she set herself free," said Deputy Franklin, walking across the hall and picking up the handcuffs and a paperclip that was lying on the floor beside them. "You left her with access to tools. What difference does it make now, anyhow? She's probably around here someplace. If not, that's her prerogative. I've got to tell you all: I'm beat, and my shift is over. I'll check back with you in the morning."

With that, both officers stepped back out into the cold night, got into their vehicles, and drove away.

Chapter 21

"*Now* what are we going to do?" Myrtle said to Klarinda and Pierre.

"I think step one is finding Benji," said Klarinda.

"It's possible she simply set herself free and is around here somewhere, not up to any trouble. Maybe finishing that bowl of ice cream," said Pierre.

"Good point," said Klarinda. "Benji!" she called. "Want to finish our game of Skip-bo?"

There was no response. Not even the creaking of a floorboard.

"We found a new jar of sprinkles for your ice cream," Myrtle tried a few seconds later.

The three of them stood frozen, waiting for several silent seconds for a response.

"We're getting our menus reprinted because you told us to," yelled Klarinda.

There was still no response.

"If that didn't get her attention, nothing will," Pierre said.

"Yep. This is what I was afraid of," said Klarinda. "I totally screwed up, and Christopher Murdock is trapped beneath an avalanche because of me."

"He very well may be guilty," said Myrtle.

"Of being in the wrong place at the wrong time," said Klarinda.

"There's nothing we can do to help him right now," said Pierre. "Right now, we need to find Benji."

"I think we should all stick together," said Myrtle.

"We'll be faster if we're all looking at once," said Pierre.

"We need to get the police back here," said Klarinda. "Whether they like it or not. This is their job, not ours."

"They haven't been much help so far," said Myrtle.

"I think they've done more harm than good," Pierre agreed.

"Fine. Let's split up, but please, you two, be careful. You're the only family I have," said Klarinda.

"We will be. You be careful, too," said Myrtle.

"Meet you both right back here in five minutes?" said Pierre.

Myrtle and Klarinda nodded. Then Pierre headed down the basement stairs, and Myrtle set off for the kitchen, leaving Klarinda to head upstairs.

Chapter 22

Klarinda had grabbed an old, sharp-tipped umbrella from the stand by the front door, and with each bedskirt she lifted, she had the umbrella poised and ready to impale Benji. But she'd made her way through each room without incident. Now she stood back in the orange room, taking one last look around it.

Benji's backpack and the guest towel and bloody leash were right where Klarinda had last seen them. She walked over to the backpack and poured out its contents.

Rust colored clothing, along with leftover remnants of the backpack's former life, piled onto the floor. Pens. A few pencils. Some ponytail holders and a tube of lip balm. A stack of small, square sticky notes with a dog-eared corner, that may have been insignificant, but immediately took Klarinda's mind straight to the note affixed to the stack of cash she'd received.

There were no keys, no cash, no phone. No wallet. Nothing to identify Benji or connect her with the world.

"Who *are* you, Benji?" Klarinda whispered. "Why are you involved in all of this?" She picked up the pens, examining them for business names or some other hint, but they were all generic. The pencils were plain, yellow, and stubby. Klarinda pushed her hair back from her face, frustrated.

"Are you okay up there?" called Myrtle.

"Yes! Coming," said Klarinda.

She left Benji's possessions in a pile and went back down the stairs. She was relieved to see both Pierre and Myrtle safely back at the front desk.

"Any sign of her?" she asked them.

They both shook their heads. "We should probably check our apartments," said Pierre.

"I think I'm going to drive around and look for her," said Klarinda. She reached under the counter, behind the stack of phone books no one ever used, expecting her hand to close around the keys for her truck. But instead, her fingers scraped against the back of the smooth wood veneer of the shelf. She pulled the phonebooks out, revealing a vacant gap of space behind them. Her keys, and the mysterious envelope of cash they'd been resting on, were gone.

"Oh, no," she said.

"What's the matter?" asked Myrtle.

Without bothering to put even a coat on, Klarinda threw open the front door and ran out to the porch of the inn. The space in front of the garage door had been haphazardly shoveled out, and there were fresh tracks from her truck going through them.

Klarinda turned and ran back inside. "She's gone," she announced.

"Gone?" Myrtle repeated.

"She stole my truck. She's escaped from here!"

"And we can't even go after her," Myrtle realized, "since the plow truck isn't drivable."

"We could try venturing out in my golf cart," Pierre suggested.

"I appreciate the offer, but we are not going to go barreling down the icy mountain in your golf cart," Klarinda said. "My truck has been stolen, and as much as they aren't going to want to hear from us again, we need to call the police. Here we go again," she said, reaching for the inn's telephone, at the exact same instant it began to ring.

"Hello?" said Klarinda.

"Hello. This is Deputy Franklin. Klarinda Snow?"

"Yes, this is she, Deputy Franklin. I was just picking up the phone to call you."

"Let me guess," he said. "You're calling to report a stolen vehicle?"

"That's right," she said. "Have you found my truck?"

"*Found* it? Well, that's one way to put it. I'm currently watching it disappear into the river."

"Disappear into the river? With Benji *inside* it?"

"She attempted to escape on foot after she jumped out of it. It crashed through the guardrail on Old Mill Road. That's where we apprehended her. She's currently in the custody of the Windy Pines police department, being interrogated by Sheriff Carter. Your truck, however, is a lost cause."

"How did you know to go after her in the first place?"

"We didn't. I only wanted to pull her over after I saw her weaving all over the road, very slowly, with her headlights turned off. When I turned my siren on, she went speeding off, and then eventually jumped from the vehicle."

"I guess she wasn't lying when she said she didn't have her driver's license," said Klarinda.

"I guess not," the deputy agreed.

"I don't know what to say," said Klarinda.

"I'm sure you're wondering how Christopher Murdock is doing," said the deputy.

Klarinda swallowed. "Is he going to be okay?"

"He's going to be fine. He's been dug out of the avalanche. There's not a scratch on him. Also, he's got two bags of salt and vinegar potato chips that he says he'd like to return to you."

"Great," Klarinda whispered. "You can tell him he can keep them," she added.

"I'll keep you posted on Benji," said the deputy, "but for now, I need to go."

"Thank you," said Klarinda, hanging up the phone.

Chapter 23

Klarinda was in Mexico, relaxing on the beach while waiting for the restoration company to complete the repairs on Mistletoe Manor when the letter from Myrtle arrived.

Dear Klarinda,

I'm glad you're getting some much deserved rest and relaxation. The inn is looking great! They just tiled the upstairs bathroom floor this morning. It looks better than I've ever seen it look! It's all really coming together nicely. You're going to be so happy when you get home, and I can tell that you'll be very comfortable there again, even after everything that happened.

Now, for some bad news. It's about Benji. It turns out, her name wasn't Benji at all. Her name was Adaline Burtz. She was Avery Burtz's older sister. (Avery is that girl from Mount Hemlock Academy who took her own life.) You're probably wondering why I'm talking about her in the past tense. Well, she also took her own life. It happened last night, when she was in a holding cell up in the county jail. I'm afraid I don't know any more details than that. I hate to even tell you this when you're on vacation, but I thought you'd want to know. I hope it doesn't ruin the rest of your time away.

It turns out that Benji/Adaline was living here in Windy Pines, right down the hill in that big old house that's been divided up into apartments. I guess that's how she got her hands on the invitations. I don't know how long she'd been living here, or much more than that about her. Maybe when you get back in town Deputy Franklin can fill you in on more details about the case. I know you didn't think very highly of him, but he sure has been asking about you!

Before I forget, because I'm certainly trying to block out the events that happened recently, I've set her backpack and its contents on the shelf in the basement of the inn. The police collected the leash and towel.

In other gossip, Pierre is enjoying his break from running the dining room, and I'm enjoying this hiatus from inn life as well. It's been great having some time off! We ought to close down for a month every year! ☺

Rod Showers and I have been seeing quite a bit of each other. I'm gaga for him! Not to mention, it looks like we might be saving some money on our plumbing repairs around the inn from now on!

I'm looking forward to seeing you when you get home. Bring me some nice seashells in your suitcase!

Love,

Myrtle

Klarinda put the letter back in its envelope and set it beneath her lounge chair. She took a deep breath, and dabbed at the unexpected stream of tears that were running down her face.

"Adeline Burtz," she said. It felt important to say it. To know Benji's real name, and to speak it aloud. Despite that she was murderer, Klarinda felt sorry for her. Just enough to shed a few tears for her. Perhaps it was unfair to the victims to sympathize so much with their murderer, but emotions didn't always follow the rules of logic.

The waves were coming in, the frothy foam reaching farther up the shoreline, lapping at Klarinda's toes. She pulled her feet back, stood up, and gathered her beach tote and the book she'd been reading. She stuck the letter from Myrtle inside it and then took a long moment to look out at the darkening ocean. She'd meant for this vacation to help her clear her head, but it was impossible to escape from the recent craziness. So she let herself wallow in it for as long as this bout wanted to stick around.

When the sun had dipped even lower and she was up to her ankles in the cool water, Klarinda brushed the last of her tears away, picked up her things, and walked back to her resort.

"Hello, Miss Snow! You're just in time for our dance party," the concierge announced when she stepped back into the main lobby.

"In my next life, my inn is going to be somewhere tropical," Klarinda decided, accepting her nightly complimentary piña colada and heading to her cabana to change into her cutest dance-off attire.

Afterword

The backpack stayed on the shelf in the basement for months, untouched. It wasn't until the morning of a spring cleaning day in April, when Klarinda woke up early and went downstairs to get started ahead of Myrtle, that she ventured to take the backpack down from its dusty perch and give it a second look.

The clothes and other items, reminders of those terrible December days, had been stuffed back inside, by either Myrtle or the police. Klarinda removed the bag's contents and set everything on top of the washing machine and dryer, spreading it all out carefully before her, looking for some further insight into the events that had transpired.

Why the penchant for rust colored clothing? she wondered. And why had the backpack been left at the inn? Had its contents been meant to be disposable, or had leaving it behind been an oversight – the result of escaping in a panicked rush?

Klarinda had been hoping the contents would lead to some huge revelation, or even some tiny, meaningful observation, but spread out beneath the dim basement lights, the clothes, pens, pencils, and other trinkets just looked like a pile of secondhand castoffs.

She sighed and gathered the smaller items back together, placing them in little pile in the bottom of the

126

backpack. Then she picked it up, ready to top it off with the clothing and put it back on the shelf. Most likely, to never be visited again. But then she paused, considering.

For a backpack that only held some pens, pencils, and ponytail holders, it was heavy. Not terribly heavy, but heavier than seemed to make sense. The last time she'd touched this bag, she'd been in a state of panicked exhaustion. But now, calm and clear-headed, she patted the bag, attempting to find some missing pocket or bulky spot. Only the base of it had any substance. She turned the bag around, searching its exterior for a zipper. There was nothing to be found. Then she looked back inside the bag, running her hand along the interior of it. And suddenly, simply, she was pulling a tiny, hidden flap, lifting the false bottom of the bag up, pushing the pens and pencils off to the side, and her fingers were brushing against something cold and smooth. Her fingers closed around a tiny antique locket on a fine, delicate chain. She pulled it out of the bag and opened it. Inside was a photo of two smiling little girls. The older one had red hair. The younger was blonde. Klarinda held the locket up to the bulb dangling from the ceiling, so she could have a closer look. *Adaline and Avery* read the miniscule engraving on the front of the locket.

She studied the photo for a moment, and then she took a deep breath, exhaled, and returned her attention to the hidden compartment of the backpack, and to a spiral bound notebook. It looked like an old, battered notebook, the likes of which she hadn't seen since her childhood. Klarinda pulled it out of the bag and flipped through it, reading the scrawling diary entries:

I'm here. It's finally happening. After all my planning. There was a time I didn't think I was strong enough to do this, but I'm proving myself wrong. I'm stronger than anyone would believe.

I can't believe it's been ten years. Can you see me, Avery? Do you know what's about to happen? <u>I'm doing this for you.</u>

You'd think I'd be excited, but I feel tired just thinking about all the work ahead of me.

They don't even have fires going in the fireplaces. The low standards of the world depress me.

There's no Christmas tree! So far, nothing is like I imagined.

I still can't believe there's no Christmas tree. I've added another name to my list and it's <u>Klarinda Snow.</u>

Victim #1 went down like butter melting in a pan. Sara never knew what hit her. And these idiots blamed it on a visit from the plumber?? This is going to be easier than I thought.

I'm feeling more excited. <u>I can do this!</u> It might even be fun.

I was going to save that idiot Tessa for last, but would you believe she managed to do herself in? It was all I could do to keep from laughing!

These radiators are so noisy! I hate this place!

I can't sleep. I might as well get some more work done.

Some sleeping pills wiped out Caroline and Jacob. Easy Peasy. With all they had to drink, it seemed like overkill. LOL.

Could they play some Christmas music around here at least? Dammit. At least they listened to me and got a Christmas tree. Klarinda Snow, you're lucky you respected my wishes. Very lucky.

Christopher was supposed to be next, but he seems immune to being poisoned. I'll have to up his dosage. With everything he's eating, it's like he's not even affected by it. What a pig.

These police are making this way too easy for me.

The Christmas tree is very pretty. Just like I imagined! I love it. XXOO

I'm going to get that little dog next. That will hurt Lannie more than dying. Ha!

You're not going to believe this. The bathtub I was reflooding miraculously broke through the floor at the same instant Lannie was untying her dog from the bed. And the dog escaped. That means I'm not an animal abuser. That's a relief. Deep in my heart, I know I'm a good person.

I'm getting a feeling that Christopher is going to try to escape. I don't really care if he stays or goes. My work here is done.

This was the last entry in the little notebook.

"Good thing Myrtle ordered that Christmas tree," Klarinda said to herself, a nervous little laugh escaping her throat.

She skimmed the entries again, wondering what, if anything, to do next. Part of her wanted to destroy the notebook. Another part wished she'd never found it. Unsure what good could come from sharing it at this point, she placed the notebook back where she'd found it. And when she did, her jaw dropped all over again.

Nestled there, perfectly wedged into the base of the bag, was the manila envelope that she'd first seen back in December. The envelope Todd Healy had delivered on the day when the mystery had all started. She pulled it from its hiding spot and turned it over in her hands a couple of times, feeling its weight. She peeked inside, confirming it truly was the stack of hundred dollar bills.

"No way," she whispered to herself, just as the basement door creaked open.

"You ready to get this party started?" asked Myrtle, coming down the stairs with a bucket of rags and cleaners.

"Ready as I'll ever be," said Klarinda, reassembling the contents of the backpack and setting them aside.

"Oh no," said Myrtle, seeing what Klarinda had been up to. "You sure you want to go down memory lane?"

"I've already been there and back."

"How was it?" asked Myrtle.

"Weird," said Klarinda.

"Did you find anything new?"

Klarinda debated this question for a moment. "New? No. I can't say I did."

"Good. Visit the past, but don't live in it. That's what I always say. Life keeps moving on, which means you have to, too. Right?"

"Right," said Klarinda. And then, without warning, she gave Myrtle a big hug.

"Well... Thanks. Are you *that* excited that I'm going to help you clean the basement?" Myrtle laughed.

"Yes. And I'm happy to have you and Pierre. I'm feeling pretty lucky right now."

"So I guess that means you're still happy to be the innkeeper of Mistletoe Manor?" asked Myrtle, passing a bottle of cleaner and a rag to Klarinda.

"I've never been happier."

"Is it because Deputy Franklin eats his lunch here nearly every day now?" asked Myrtle, winking.

"No! Although he's not as bad as I thought. Mainly, it's because of how business is going. Having everything remodeled and updated has eased a lot of stress. And who would have thought that everything that happened would actually make us more popular?"

"Things are good," Myrtle agreed. "And I've never been happier either." She sighed, admiring the engagement ring Rod Showers had given her two weeks earlier.

"Have you two set a date?" asked Klarinda.

"Soon, if we can have the wedding here at the inn," Myrtle suggested, smiling hopefully.

"I think we can arrange that," Klarinda said.

"Are you serious?"

"Of course, Myrtle. This inn has been your home for years. If you want to have your wedding here, you really don't even need to ask me."

"Well, thank you," Myrtle said, her eyes growing misty. "I swear," she said, dabbing at her eyes, and laughing, "We're nothing but a couple of crybabies."

"It's okay," said Klarinda.

"I *told* you this place was destined for more happy times," Myrtle declared. "Didn't I tell you that?"

Klarinda laughed. "At least a couple of times. And as usual, Myrtle, you really *do* know what you're talking about. I may never doubt you again."

Thank you to Katie Ripley and Taya Curtis for your excellent proofing skills and helpful feedback. And thanks to my husband Bill for being the very first reader of every book I write, as well as my most supportive fan!

Thanks for reading Murder at Mistletoe Manor! Please take a moment to leave a review.

A note about the author:

Holly Tierney-Bedord lives in Madison, Wisconsin. She is the author of several books including the novels and novellas *Bellamy's Redemption, Right Under Your Nose, Surviving Valencia, Run Away Baby,* and *Coached.*

Sign up for Holly's free eNewsletter by visiting www.hollytierneybedord.com to receive first looks, freebies, discounts, and news!

About *Surviving Valencia:*

Twins Van and Valencia Loden are killed in a tragic accident shortly after they start college. Charmed, bright, and beautiful, they held their family together and elevated their family to greatness. In their loss, a shadow is cast upon the family, particularly on the remaining child, who lacks the easy grace and popularity her older siblings took for granted.

As an adult, her life begins to turn from mediocre to amazing when she is saved by cool, artistic Adrian. The kind of happiness once reserved only for others is finally hers, until pieces of the past begin ruining what seems to be a perfect life.

Enjoy the following free preview of **Right Under Your Nose: A Christmas Story.**

Right Under Your Nose ~ Chapter 1

"I hope you haven't gotten me a present yet, because I'm not celebrating Christmas this year."

"You're kidding."

"No," said Ariadne. "I'm one hundred percent serious."

"You're not exchanging gifts, or you're not celebrating it at all?" asked Jess.

"I'm not celebrating it at all. No tree, no stocking, no gifts, no Christmas cookies. And definitely no caroling!"

"But you love those things!"

"Let me continue," said Ariadne. "No goofy Christmas sweaters, no Christmas music, no sledding parties, no glittery snow globes."

"So are you forgoing Christmas or the entire season of winter?"

"I haven't decided yet."

"You really mean to tell me that you're going to let Scott make a decision like that for you?" asked Jess.

"What's that supposed to mean?" asked Ariadne. She'd been about to take a sip of her coffee, but she set the mug back down on the table.

"I mean, Scott breaks up with you, and…"

"For the record, that's not what happened," Ariadne said.

"If you'd tell me the details, I wouldn't have to speculate," said Jess.

"I'll tell you someday."

"Fine. So, you and Scott break up, and the next thing I know, you're going to Grinch it this year."

"Grinch it. You're hilarious. I'm not in a state to celebrate. I'm depressed. Okay? Is it that hard for you to understand?"

"I get that you're depressed, Ariadne, but do you really think pouting all winter long and skipping your favorite holiday is going to cheer you up?"

"You wouldn't understand."

"Why do you say that?" asked Jess. He scratched his beard and took a sip of his tea. He raised an eyebrow at Ariadne, waiting.

"Because you're not emotional."

"I am too."

"Not really."

"I *can* be."

Ariadne rolled her eyes and took a sip of her coffee, not bothering to respond to that.

"So," said Jess, "when *are* you going to tell me what happened with you two? You're Madison's two most famous chefs. You seemed like a match made in heaven."

"We're two of many, and we were never a match made in heaven. Did you see that article in the paper?"

"I'd be lying if I said no."

"I can't believe that bitchy reporter Gabby Gaffney wrote about us splitting up. As if that's newsworthy. She actually called me at work and attempted to interview me. The nerve! She had all these awful, invasive questions. Really personal stuff that was none of her business!"

"How bizarre for a reporter to ask invasive questions," said Jess.

"Shut up! I told her I had nothing to say, but she managed to write about us anyway."

"At least Scott didn't talk to her either," said Jess.

"How big of him."

"I guess it shows you're the success story you always wanted to be."

"I never wanted to be some 'success story' or whatever you want to call it; I just wanted to be successful. There's a difference."

Jess laughed. "I remember coming home from college, sitting around the Thanksgiving table with our families, and there you were, all ready to be the next... I don't know. Gordon Ramsay? Paula Dean?"

"Hilarious! Actually, I wanted to be the next Giada De Laurentiis, but more baker-ish."

"My point exactly. When it was your turn to say what you were thankful for, you said, 'I'm thankful I'm in culinary school, and acing all my classes, and on the path to becoming a super big deal.'"

"I was never that obnoxious."

"It wasn't obnoxious. It was intimidating! I was about to flunk out and there you were, setting the bar way too high, as usual," said Jess.

"Well, the bar is pretty low for me now, and you're doing great. Things have a funny way of balancing out."

"You'll get over Scott. You will. It'll just take some time."

Ariadne shook her head. "Let's talk about something else. How are you and that new girl you've been dating? What's her name? Lauren?"

"Laurel."

"How long have you two been together now?"

"Since September."

"Two whole months! That must be a record for you."

"Now who's the funny one," said Jess. He dunked one of Ariadne's biscotti sticks in his tea and bit it in half.

"Quit stealing," she said, hitting his hand. "On second thought, have it. It reminds me of him."

"Did you two bake a lot of biscotti together?" asked Jess.

"No. The name. Biscotti. It's too close to Scotty. I'm done with it."

"Cool. More for me," said Jess.

"So, back to Laurel. Have you two moved in together yet?"

"Her toothbrush is in my bathroom, if that's what you're wondering."

"She's brushes her teeth. That's good. What's she like? I can't believe I haven't met her yet."

"She's great."

"But not great like me, right?"

"Glad to see you haven't lost your confidence."

"I'm trying hard to keep it at an uncomfortable level. Just for you."

"Thanks," Jess said, laughing.

Ariadne leaned closer to him and lowered her voice. "In reality," she said, "I feel like a total loser. I can tell you that, right?"

"Sure. You can tell me anything."

"I know! Usually I abuse that rule."

"Hey," Jess said.

"Hey what? Uh oh. Why do you look all serious?" asked Ariadne.

"You can tell me whatever you want to tell me, when you want to. About what happened with you two, I mean. Or, if you don't want to, that's okay too."

"I know I can tell you. I will soon. Not today, though."

"Okay," said Jess. He finished the biscotti. "I'm doing you a favor. Getting it out of your way," he explained.

"Right. Thanks. So, are you bringing her to our Thanksgiving dinner next week?"

"I might. Will you be there? Or have you decided to boycott every holiday?"

"I'll be there. I promised our moms I'd help them with dessert. If I hadn't already made that promise, I'd be hiding out at home, watching movies, alone."

"Well, in that case, I'm glad you made that promise." Jess glanced at his watch. "Speaking of Laurel, I need to pick her up from play practice."

"So soon?"

"We've been talking for two and a half hours!"

"I suppose I'd better go, too," said Ariadne. She didn't move though.

Jess downed the rest of his tea, stood up, gave Ariadne a quick kiss on the cheek, and zipped up his down parka. "Are you coming?" he asked.

"I'm just going to finish my coffee. You go ahead."

"Okay. See you next week. Your mom's hosting this year, right?"

Ariadne nodded. "See you then."

She took another sip of her cold coffee and watched Jess stepping out the coffee shop door, going to the corner, and crossing the street. She drew in a deep breath and sighed.

"Can I take this away from you?" asked a young woman with a tub of dirty dishes. She pointed at Jess's empty mug on the table.

"Sure, thanks," said Ariadne. The woman put the mug in her tub and swiped at the table with a damp cloth. She then replaced a vase of fake flowers and a sandwich menu that Jess had set on a neighboring table. She topped off the table with a glass bear of honey, a basket of sugar packets, and a printout in a tall, plastic holder advertising an upcoming poetry slam,. By the time she walked away, Ariadne felt like she was barricaded behind a wall.

It's like I'm not even here, Ariadne wrote on her napkin. She read the words a few times and then added *I wish someone cared about me.* After she'd spent a couple of minutes feeling appropriately sorry for herself, but not so sad that she started crying in public, she wadded up the napkin and tossed it into a nearby plant. She took her phone out of her purse and trying to entertain herself. Nothing was happening in her virtual world. Why would it be? It was four o'clock in the afternoon on a Monday.

She glanced around the assortment of tchotchkes on the table to the space Jess had just occupied, imagining for a second that he might have remanifested himself there, but there was nothing but an empty chair. The coffee shop was almost completely empty, and getting bleaker all the time. Ariadne decided the removal of his mug was what had caused this chain of reactions and the only option now was to leave. She stood up and pulled on her coat.

Back in the spring, buying a gigantic Victorian house had seemed like a great idea. She hadn't listened to one word of warning from her naysaying friends and family:

"It'll cost so much to heat it!"

"Why do you need a six bedroom house?"

"It'll be too much work!"

"It's a total fixer-upper! Buy a condo instead!"

She'd been *so* proud of herself for finding such a great deal in one of Madison's most desirable neighborhoods.

At the time, she and Scott were still together. Before she bought her house, they'd spent the majority of their time together at his apartment since hers was so tiny. His place, filled with bizarre quirks like an accordion door on the bathroom and a tacky chandelier dripping in fake pearls, had been her second home. She'd gotten her mail there. It had been more of a home to her than her own apartment. So when she bought her house, she'd figured soon it could be his house, too. Just as she'd migrated into his larger, more comfortable space, he'd do the same with hers.

In her imaginings, they'd remodel the kitchen into a chef's paradise. They'd plant an amazing garden, filled with herbs and berries and every kind of vegetable. Someday they'd fill the house with kids.

But this wasn't how it had turned out. Once she'd moved into her house, Scott had stayed as planted in his apartment as ever. She'd taken her time moving her things out, since the time they spent together was almost exclusively on his turf. Despite her telling him that he could spend as much time in her new home as he'd like, this notion had never quite taken.

Now, without him, her house stood as a giant, drafty, spooky reminder of just how alone she was. With winter setting in, all her extra money was going to heat it, just as everyone had predicted. She was realizing she'd made a big mistake.

Lately, this was her fortune. One mistake after another. The days of being a success seemed to be all in the past.

Right Under Your Nose ~ Chapter 2

Halfway through her short walk home, Ariadne stopped in her tracks, in front of a bookstore that seemed to have sprung up overnight. *Right Under Your Nose* read the wooden sign hanging in front of the door. She cupped her mittened hands around her face and peeked in the front window. The shelves inside were filled with thousands of books, haphazardly stacked and leaning in precariously tilting piles. It looked like the kind of place that had existed for fifty years. But that was impossible. She'd lived in her house since May, and she'd known this neighborhood for years. She certainly would know this shop if it had been here all along.

She opened the door, jingling a string of bells hanging from it as she went inside.

"Greetings," said the old man sitting behind the front desk.

"Hi," said Ariadne. She looked around and took in a deep breath of the magical smell of old books, mingling with the welcoming aroma of cookies and cider.

"What brings you in today?" asked the man.

"Well... The cold, for one thing; it looked so warm and inviting in here. I've never seen this place before. Are you new?"

"New?" asked the old man. He chuckled. "No. I've been here since 1968."

"You have? I live just two blocks from here. I'm not sure how I never noticed you before."

"I'm tucked back from the street a little. Easy to miss."

"I could have sworn this place was a... never mind."

"What were you saying?" he asked.

Ariadne shook her head, feeling flustered. "Was this ever a yoga studio? Have you always been right here, in this exact same location?"

"Since 1968."

"I guess I need to pay more attention," she said.

"Help yourself to some hot apple cider," said the man, "and some pumpkin cookies. My wife Margie's special recipe. Let me know if you need any help finding anything. I admit, my organizing system might not be the easiest to understand, but I can usually help folks find what they're searching for."

"Thank you," said Ariadne. There was a little sign taped to the back of the cash register, right above the cookie plate, telling customers to *Please Take a Cookie.*

"This place is adorable. I really don't know how I've missed it," she said to the man.

"I'm glad you like it. We always tried to make it homey."

"It is! It definitely is."

"Thank you," said the man. He smiled, but his eyes looked sad. "If you'll excuse me," he said, heading toward the back of the shop.

Ariadne nibbled the cookie, careful to keep crumbs off the books, while she perused the shelves. The cookie practically melted in her mouth. *I need to see the recipe for this,* she decided with the rare urgency usually reserved for moments when she was dining at a particularly delicious competitor's restaurant.

She finished it, dusted off her fingertips, and was about to go back for another when a book called *Decorating Your Victorian Home for the Holidays* caught her eye. It rested under a crooked *Non-Fiction: How-To Section* sign, atop a pile of books about caring for houseplants, training puppies, and restoring antique tractors. Momentarily forgetting her plan to skip Christmas, Ariadne picked it up and began flipping through it.

The pages were thick and glossy. Page after page of inspiration. There were stockings hanging on tall mantels. Tall fir trees adorned in ribbons and softly glittering angels. Evergreen boughs wound their way up grand banisters and sidewalks twinkled with rows of old lanterns set in the snow. Ariadne sighed.

"Two dollars," said the old man.

"Oh! I didn't realize you were right there." Ariadne set the book back where she'd found it.

"Didn't mean to sneak up on you. So, that's not the book for you? Usually I'm so good at this! Victorian houses aren't your thing after all?"

"It's not that," said Ariadne. "It's just... I'm not celebrating Christmas. Not this year, anyway."

"Not celebrating Christmas this year? I'm sorry to hear that."

"Never mind. I really didn't mean to burden you with my problems."

"You're not burdening me. I admit, I can see where you're coming from."

"You can?"

The old man nodded. "Ever since Margie passed away, I haven't felt quite the same about the holidays. I bake her cookies because they make me feel like she's still close to me... But sometimes... Well... I get it. I get where you're coming from." The old man's eyes filled with tears. He looked down self-consciously.

"I can see you really do understand. Thanks," said Ariadne. She hesitated, unsure what to say. She didn't want to upset the man further, but changing the subject seemed kind of harsh. "You two were together a long time?" she asked.

The man nodded. "You could say that. Our whole lives. We grew up right next door to each other."

"That's amazing," Ariadne said.

"Why don't you take that book with you," said the man. "No charge. Just take it. I think you'll like it."

"I'll pay you," Ariadne said, opening her purse.

"No, no. Please, take it."

Ariadne smiled. "If you insist, then sure. Thank you." She tucked it under her arm. "I suppose I'd better get home. Nice place you've got here. I'll stop by again soon."

"That would be nice. Would you like a cookie for the road?"

"Don't mind if I do," she said.

The old man wrapped two in a napkin and gave them to her. "You have a good night," he said.

"You too," said Ariadne, feeling cheerier than she had in days.

End of free sample.

25115147R00086

Printed in Great Britain
by Amazon